Dillon watched again as Jovan occupied Aimee's attention.

He wished he knew if she was just being nice to him or if she actually enjoyed his company. Jovan had a carefree charisma that women seemed to be drawn to.

Dillon knew that he had no such charisma. One couldn't plan charisma. And if it couldn't be planned, he couldn't do it.

"You watch her from a distance long enough, and one of these times you'll watch her walk right out of your life."

He turned and considered Katie's words.

She elbowed him. "What are you waiting for? If you like her, tell her."

Like didn't cover the gamut of emotions Aimee rocked in him. The one pulling out in front most would be labeled as *love*. But could Aimee be happy with him? He wasn't a free spirit like her. . .and Jove. He was bound by his plans. If he didn't plan, he felt lost. He felt lost without Aimee, too. But most of all, he wanted Aimee to be happy in her life. . .even if that life was without him.

MARY DAVIS is a full-time writer whose first published novel was *Newlywed Games* from Multnomah. She enjoys going into schools and talking to kids about writing. Mary lives near Colorado's Rocky Mountains with her husband, three children, and six pets.

Books by Mary Davis

HEARTSONG PRESENTS

Don't miss out on any of our super romances. Write to us at the following address for information on our newest releases and club information.

Heartsong Presents Readers' Service
PO Box 721
Uhrichsville, OH 44683

Or visit www.heartsongpresents.com

The Grand Hotel

Mary Davis

Heartsong Presents

Dedicated to my mom, Zola. Let's plan a trip.

And to the men and women who work at the Grand and make it grand indeed.

And a special thanks to Ken Hayward and Stacie Ellison at the Grand.

And thanks to Jan for the riddle help.

A note from the Author:
I love to hear from my readers! You may correspond with me by writing:

Mary Davis
Author Relations
PO Box 721
Uhrichsville, OH 44683

ISBN 1-59310-879-6

THE GRAND HOTEL

Scripture taken from the HOLY BIBLE, NEW INTERNATIONAL VERSION ®. NIV ®. Copyright © 1973, 1978, 1984 by International Bible Society. Used by permission of Zondervan Publishing House. All rights reserved.

All of the characters and events in this book are fictitious. Any resemblance to actual persons, living or dead, or to actual events is purely coincidental.

Our mission is to publish and distribute inspirational products offering exceptional value and biblical encouragement to the masses.

PRINTED IN THE U.S.A.

one

I'm almost there, Nonie.

Aimee Mikkelson stood at the bow of the foot-passenger ferry's top deck. The wind whipped at her green plaid capris and lime green T-shirt and pulled at her shoulder-length blond hair.

Mackinac Island loomed closer with each passing minute.

She had grown up with the romantic tales of when her great-great-grandfather Adam Wright helped build the island's largest hotel. The size of the construction crew had matched the massive structure they were trying to build in the span of a few short months. Adam Wright had become smitten with the daughter of one of the crew chiefs, and though interested, Lacey had resisted his charms. . .for a while.

Aimee's breath caught, and her heart seemed to stop as she realized the large white structure that stretched against the green hillside of Mackinac Island was her destination—the Grand Hotel.

Now she just needed to figure out how to get inside and search the hotel. She only had two days. She had found the cheapest room on the island, which wasn't all that cheap but was of those available during the busy tourist season. Memorial Day weekend was not the time to book a last-minute trip. But she was afraid Nonie's health couldn't wait. Blind, diabetic, and now a broken hip. Aimee had heard of old people going into the hospital for something as simple as a broken bone and developing pneumonia, or worse, and dying. The realization that this could be the end for Nonie had broken Aimee's heart and spurred her on in her quest. Nonie had said it was fine to let the secret die and only the two of them would believe it was really there. But she knew Nonie's heart; Nonie had always wanted to find the treasure in the Grand Hotel but had given up on finding it because no one else believed in the family legend. Nonie had found a coconspirator in Aimee, and they had sat and dreamed about what treasure awaited them. The idea of the treasure seemed to grow over the years, to where now they would laugh about whether the two of them could carry it.

Aimee had two goals after graduating from high school: find her prodigal older sister—which she did, along with a fourteen-year-old nephew, Justin—and help Nonie get to Mackinac Island. Even if they found no treasure, Nonie would at least get to experience the hotel. Now Aimee needed to find whatever Nonie's grandfather had left his descendants. Even if Nonie couldn't see it, she could hold it in her hands and feel the special connection to her ancestor Adam Wright who cared enough about his loved ones that he would leave behind a secret legacy.

The ferry slowed and turned toward the pier that jutted out from the small town on the edge of the water. Aimee could no longer see the great white hotel, so she descended the two flights of stairs with the other passengers who were preparing to disembark.

A group of women came up behind her talking. "Madison and Huey are so lucky to be getting married on Mackinac Island. It's so romantic."

"And at the Grand Hotel, no less. That's where I want to get married some day."

Adam and Lacey had been married on the island. Aimee

thought it would be romantic to be married in the very place they said their vows. Nonie always remarked that Aimee had the same enthusiasm for life as her granddad Adam.

The ferry docked, and Aimee stepped off with the other passengers. A surge of energy passed through her as her feet touched the island for the first time. She waited for her two rolling suitcases to be unloaded and looped her purse and camera case over one of the handles. She asked for directions from one of the ferry workers as to where the Island House was located and headed off the pier toward her hotel. She passed by the gals she had heard talking on the ferry as they climbed aboard a maroon, hard-shelled carriage with *Grand Hotel* embossed in gold on the side. She may not be taking a fancy horse-drawn coach, but she'd get inside the Grand just the same.

After checking in at the Island House and dropping off her luggage, she changed into one of the three dresses she'd brought along, a short-sleeved red one with large white polka dots. She looked in the mirror and spun around. The full skirt fluttered like a flag in a strong breeze. After 6 p.m., a dress was required for all women in the Grand Hotel and a coat and tie for the men. And since it was already midafternoon, she could very well be there until after six. She didn't want to chance getting kicked out for not following the rules. . .that was, if she managed to get inside.

How she was going to get inside to look around was her first problem. The hotel had become such a tourist attraction that a fee was required for nonhotel guests, so the hotel guests could enjoy the accommodations they paid for. She could pay the entrance fee to walk on the premises but didn't think that would afford her the freedom she needed to really look around inside. The porch and grounds were not of interest to her.

Lord, like the woman who lost a coin and searched her house from top to bottom until she found it, I, too, will search for Nonie's inheritance. I'm sure it is meant to be found. Help me find it. And please give me a way into the Grand Hotel that will allow me the latitude to look freely until I find it. Then I, too, will rejoice in finding what was lost.

She looped her white cardigan over her arm and headed out for the Grand.

　　　　　　　　　　　　　❧

Dillon Thurough watched the perky blond conversing with the doorman. Was she one of those tourists who thought she could sweet-talk her way in without paying the entrance fee? Did she belong here? She looked like trouble to him. Not that he thought she was really trouble, but deep down he had a strange feeling she'd be trouble for him. As one of the assistant managers of the Grand Hotel, diverting or diffusing trouble was his job.

He adjusted his navy blue suit coat and strode toward Henry at the entrance. Henry was in his early seventies with a white mustache. He wore a traditional red double-breasted beefeater uniform with a black top hat. Rumor had it he'd been with the hotel for over half a century. "Is there a problem?"

"No, sir." Henry gave him a slow dip of his head.

The blond turned her bright smile on him and shoved out her hand. "Hi, I'm Aimee Mikkelson."

Now that was a great smile. Like sunshine. The kind of smile that could get a guy to do anything a gal wanted. But not this guy. He untangled his thoughts from her smile and shook her outstretched hand, her grip firm, her hand soft. He had a weakness for blonds, but he could control it and school his initial attraction. Knowing one's weakness made temptation easier to resist.

She went on. "Henry has been great. He was just telling me

how to find the wedding festivities. I can't tell you how excited I am to be here. This place is like a dream, like a fairy tale."

He forced himself to focus on the conversation and not the way her wavy golden hair framed her cute round face. "You're with the Dodson-Whitehall party?"

"I'm taking pictures for Madison and Huey." She pointed to the black bag slung over her shoulder that looked like it could be a camera bag.

That sounded fishy. "We have a hotel photographer who'll be taking the wedding photos."

"Oh, I'm not doing any of the formal wedding pics. I'm taking candid shots of the bride and groom, family and friends, to give a broader perspective of Maddy's special day." Her hands moved back and forth as she spoke. "It's one thing to have the beautiful portraits to remember this once-in-a-lifetime moment, but it's another to have that unique shot of Aunt Millie not only talking to the colonel but actually laughing at one of his bad jokes. Or catching Tommy putting a frog in Julie's purse. Those are once-in-a-lifetime treasures beyond measure. Something to show their grandchildren."

He believed her up to that last statement, but he had no cause to deny her access to the premises at this point. "Very well. There is a reception on the west lawn in half an hour, then a dinner at seven in the dining room."

Her smile broadened. "You're a peach. Thanks. I'm just going to wander in here for a few until people start to gather outside."

He watched her sashay away, the hem of her red dress swishing back and forth below her knees.

"That one's a looker, she is."

He turned to Henry. "I'm not interested."

Henry smiled. "I never said you was. Only said she's a looker."

And likely trouble. He turned and walked around behind the front desk. "Katie, can I squeeze in here a minute?"

Katie stepped aside from the computer and continued to help a guest.

He put his fingers to the keyboard. He could use the computer in his office, but then he couldn't keep one eye on the perky blond with more words than a hurricane has wind. He typed in *Amy Mickelson* and every variation of its spelling he could think of. Ms. Mikkelson was not registered at the hotel. Although that fact, in and of itself, wasn't necessarily a cause for concern. Many of the wedding guests weren't staying at this hotel.

But if Ms. Mikkelson was out to cause trouble, he wanted to be close by to deal with the problem. What if she was an ex-girlfriend or ex-fiancée of the groom? Things could only get ugly. If that were the case, her only reason for being here would be to cause trouble this weekend. He was definitely sticking close to her.

❧

Aimee stood at the end of the lobby. *Yes, Lord, I know, thou shalt not lie. I didn't mean to. It just came out. My big mouth has gotten me into trouble again. But I promise I'll do everything I can to make this right.*

She sighed and turned her attention to the window and gazed out to the west. Though the lawns looked beautiful, nothing out there held any interest for her. What she needed was inside these walls. . .in the floor, to be exact.

"In a grand hall, walk west to the wall, you tread to the treasure, a gift without measure. Then north you must turn, for the prize you will earn, at the closet humble and low, a treasure in the wood below."

Family legend had it that Adam Wright hid something in

the floor of the Grand Hotel for his grandchildren. And Nonie was the only living grandchild left. Aimee had planned to bring Nonie to the hotel, but she had broken her hip and was relegated to a bed for now, with words of these being her last days and regrets of not getting to the Grand Hotel before she died. But Nonie was never in a position to come on her own. Since the age of twenty-five, Aimee's current age, Nonie had been blind. Granddad and her two children always put the story aside as a fairy tale.

Maybe Aimee could sneak down the hall and find the answers to the riddle. If she found what she was looking for today, she could be back to Nonie with it tomorrow—after she took pictures for the bride and groom, of course. She turned to see if she could go find this great hall, but the handsome assistant manager was practically on top of her, and she almost stepped into him. "Oops."

"Ms. Mikkelson." He took a step backward, straightening his navy suit jacket. His light brown hair was parted on the side and came down onto his forehead.

She hated being called "Miz." The salutation was so communal and remote. . .and formal. "It's Aimee."

"Aimee." His mouth spread into a nice smile, and his dimples tucked into each cheek.

Not dimples. Dimples were so cute and irresistible. She just wanted to poke her finger into them. She would simply have to ignore them. "What does the D stand for?" She pointed to his nametag: D. THUROUGH.

His green eyes locked on her. "Dillon."

"May I call you Dillon?"

"If you would like. I'm heading down to the west lawn. I'll show you the way."

Ah yes, the west lawn. That was where she was supposed to

be but not where she wanted to be. She had said she would take pictures so she suspected this was as good a time as any to take some, and then maybe Mr. Cute Dimples would leave her alone. He was suspicious, and though there was minor cause, she wasn't going to harm anything at the hotel—lift an already loose board, find Nonie's inheritance, and put the board back in place—so he really needn't worry. If going down and taking a few pictures would put his fears to rest, then so be it. "I would love an escort."

They walked through the lobby and out onto the porch that stretched across the entire front of the building. White wicker rocking chairs lined the length of it, as well as dozens upon dozens of red geraniums potted along the front railing. "This is some porch."

"Six hundred and sixty feet. The world's longest porch."

"Wow!" She marched down the steps with him. "The red of the geraniums really looks great against the white building."

"They are the hotel's signature flower."

"Really. Has anyone ever counted them?"

"Twenty-five hundred on the porch alone, and more around the grounds."

"Whoa. That's a lot of potting soil."

"You don't want to know."

This guy was full of tidbits of hotel trivia. "How many chairs?"

He greeted a man dressed in a red uniform like Henry's standing behind a podium thing near the bottom of the stairs. "One hundred."

"Do you ever come out here and just sit or watch the sunset."

"No!"

His swift, sharp word made her flinch.

Dillon halted her with an arm swung out in front of her.

A horse-drawn carriage rolled past them with a *cloppity-clomp* and their harnesses jingling. "The horses have the right-of-way on the island." The curtness of his statement seemed to be a reflection of his harshly spoken no.

"Why is that?"

He paused a moment. "I suppose it is because it takes longer to stop a horse than it does a person. And in a collision, the horse would win." He walked her across the narrow, paved road that ran in front of the hotel, then down the multitiered staircase to the lower grounds. An array of lilacs, honeysuckles, and spireas lined both sides. "Do you have a room at this hotel?"

"I'm staying at a place in town. That's not a problem, is it?"

"Certainly not." The staircase split halfway down. Dillon guided her to the right.

She pondered his swift answer to her question about him sitting on the porch and watching the sunset. It was a sharp contrast to what seemed to be his habit of pausing for a second or two before he spoke—the time it took to draw in a breath. Why did he guard his words? And why did the sunset momentarily cause him to drop that guard? There was always more to a person than met the eye. There was certainly more to her—if people could get past the blond stereotype. What was behind his carefully chosen words and irresistible dimples?

She stepped onto the velvet carpet of grass at the bottom of the stairs and turned around to look back up at the hotel. The hotel her great-great-grandfather had a hand in building. "It's breathtaking." Though the lawns were gorgeous and the sunshine divine, she just wanted to run back up the stairs and inside.

"It was built in only three months."

She turned to him. "You're kidding?" Adam had worked fast to win Lacey's heart.

Dillon showed her to the activity on the west lawn. "I hope you take many memories for the bride and groom." He left her at the edge of the gathering, and she approached beautifully dressed, white linen–draped tables. The wait staff looked like cookie-cutter replicas of each other: all the women dressed in black dresses with white aprons, collars, and little hats; the men in black pants, coat, and tie, with a white shirt.

What a life to live this way all the time— fine food and people waiting to serve you.

Since she said she was here to take pictures for the bride and groom, she might as well get started. Telling Henry the doorman and then one of the managers that that was what she was here for was as good as a promise to her. But all she really needed to do was snap a few shots and get an e-mail address for either Madison or Huey so she could send them the pictures, and her obligation would be fulfilled. Then she could get on with her real work here.

She glanced over at Dillon, who was speaking to one of the wait staff. In the sunlight, she could see natural reddish highlights in his light brown hair. He smiled at her, and she smiled back. She had to quit looking at his dimpled cheeks. She slipped her camera out of her bag and approached the first table. Most of the tables were still empty, but people were trickling toward them. At this table sat the three girls in their early twenties she had overheard talking on the ferry and a young man about their same age. "I'm taking pictures for the bride and groom. May I take yours so they can always remember this day and who was here to celebrate it with them?" The foursome scooted together, and she captured them in time. Somehow it seemed appropriate for her first picture to be of the girls who unknowingly gave her the opening to get inside the Grand Hotel.

She moved to the next occupied table and did the same. Then she glanced over at Dillon. He was staring at her again. She smiled and waved. He gave her a nod and turned back to the plump, red-haired woman who was talking to him. She took shots of several more groups and some individuals who had begun to gather.

Her attention was drawn to a man roaming from table to table. He couldn't have been any taller than her at five-foot-six. He had short curly brown hair. She heard him say, "Have you seen my bride?"

Aha. She'd just found Huey.

Someone at the table Huey stood beside said, "Have you lost her already? You aren't even married yet."

Huey shrugged and stood a little longer to talk; then he left that table, but before he could engage the next table with his inquiry, Aimee intercepted him.

"Huey." He turned to her, and she continued. "I'm Aimee, and I'll be taking some candid shots of the people here for your big day if that is all right with you."

"Mad would love that. She already has one scrapbook full and is planning dozens more."

"Great. Would you mind if I got your e-mail address so I can just e-mail them to you?"

"That would work super. I'll be able to just print them right off, and Mad can put them in her books."

Aimee pulled a piece of folded notebook paper out of her camera bag but couldn't find a pen. "Do you have a pen?"

Huey pulled one from his pants pocket, took the paper, and wrote down an e-mail address. "There you go. I'll look forward to hearing from you."

"Huey Dodson. Are you giving girls your phone number already?"

A young woman, about five-foot-two, scooted up next to Huey and looped her arm through his. Flyaways of her brown kinky shoulder-length hair danced in the air. Her short frame held an extra thirty to forty pounds.

"Mad, you know I'm only mad about you." Huey squeezed her hand wrapped around his arm.

Madison's mouth broke into a wide smile. "I just love it when he calls me that."

"Mad, this is Aimee. She's going to be taking pictures of people just milling around. I just gave her my e-mail addy so she can send the shots to us."

Aimee held out the paper to show her. She was about to tell Madison that if it was a problem, she would gladly return the address. The last thing she wanted to do was cause trouble between the bride and groom.

Madison's eyes widened. "Really! Oh, Huey, you did this for me?" She gave him a big hug.

Huey winked at Aimee over Madison's shoulder. She smiled and winked back to let him know she wouldn't tell his bride it wasn't his idea. Let him be the hero. That's how it should be.

Madison pulled away and playfully swatted Huey's arm. "And you who are always complaining about all my pictures." Madison turned toward Aimee. "He'll thank me one day when we're old and all we can remember of our lives are the images captured forever in fading photographs."

She had thought the glowing bride thing was just a myth. But if anyone could be considered glowing, it was Madison. And with the love shining in her eyes, she was going to make the most beautiful bride. Madison was what being a bride was all about. And the best part was the love in Huey's eyes for his bride. "I wish you both the best and a long and happy life together." She tucked the paper into her camera bag.

She was about to leave when Madison thrust a disposable camera at her. "Would you take our picture?"

Aimee took the camera and snapped the picture. The opulence of a Grand Hotel wedding in contrast with the disposable camera hit her funny, and she almost laughed. Instead, she handed back the camera and held up hers. "Let me get one of you with my camera, as well." They posed again with the Mackinac Bridge in the background, then were off with their guests.

She sighed and sent up a silent prayer that their marriage would make it for the long haul. And she sensed it would.

Now that she had accomplished everything she had said she would, her initial fib was now the truth. She could go back inside and complete another task that she had promised. She turned to walk back up the stairs to the hotel but stopped at the sound of her name.

Dillon was at her side in a few strides. "You aren't leaving so soon, are you?"

"I was just going in to use the ladies' room."

"I'm heading back inside. I'll walk with you."

She just couldn't get rid of this guy. Under other circumstances, she would love his attention, would crave his attention. But not today. But she could enjoy his company on the way back up. . .as long as she didn't look at his dimples. "Why did you come to this hotel to work?"

"Who wouldn't want to work at the Grand?"

"Well, I don't know, maybe someone who has a fear of water. After all, there is water all the way around the island." *Duh. Kind of the definition of an island.* That had sounded so. . .so dumb-blondish. "Someone who doesn't want to part with a special car. No cars allowed here. Or someone who wants to travel to other parts of the world. There could be a lot of reasons, and there are a lot of exceptional hotels like this one around the world. So why this one?"

Dillon provided the now-expected pause, then said, "I like it here."

"There has to be more to it than that, and I'm going to keep probing until I find out the answer." She suspected he was a private man by the way he guarded his words; maybe that threat would make him steer clear of her, and she could do what she came to do. "Well, thank you for escorting me back. If you could just tell me where I might find the ladies' room, I'll be out of your way." *Or you'll be out of mine.*

two

Aimee sat on the edge of the bed in her hotel room and flopped backward with her arms splayed. The day had been a total waste. She hadn't expected to find what she was looking for on the first day, but she had at least expected to make progress. She had to make progress tomorrow because she could only keep this room one more night after tonight.

Dillon Thurough had been like superglue, supercute superglue. Every time she turned around, he was there. If she could avoid the cute assistant manager with the irresistible dimples, she could make progress tomorrow, even if she didn't find what she was looking for. Then maybe she could check out of her room here early Sunday morning, attend services at The Little Stone Church near the Grand Hotel, and find what she needed on Sunday, either before or after the wedding.

She paused in her thinking. Or maybe, better yet, during the wedding? Everyone would be preoccupied with the wedding, and she could possibly slip through the hotel undisturbed. Well, maybe not everyone, but everyone of consequence— specifically Dillon Thurough.

Aimee picked up the phone and dialed the nursing home. It would be another expense to draw on her limited funds, but Nonie needed to know she had been inside the hotel and was hopeful.

A tired voice came through the line. "EagleView Assisted Living and Retirement Center, nurses' station, this is Betty speaking."

"Hi, Betty. This is Aimee Mikkelson. How's Nonie doing today?"

"She had a good day. Her hip seems to be healing as well as can be expected. If she continues to behave and do what we tell her, she should heal fine with no lasting problems."

She took a deep breath. "Is she still talking about dying?"

"She mentions it. I think she's trying to prepare you for the inevitable. She's mentally ready to die, but I don't think she has given up."

"I just don't want to think about what life will be like when she's gone."

"But one day, it will happen."

"I know." She rubbed her face. "I realize it's late, but is she still awake?"

"Sorry. The doctor ordered some strong meds to ease her pain, and they knocked her out."

"Okay. Tell her I called and I wish her well."

"She'll be sad she missed you. She sure looks forward to it when you come or call."

"Tell her I'll try to call tomorrow night, earlier. And, hopefully, I'll be back in a few days." She hung up the phone. There were plenty of family members to keep Nonie company, but none of them could find two spare minutes to give her. After Aimee found her nephew, Justin, he had been happy to visit Nonie with her.

✿

Dillon loosened his blue and gray tie and unbuttoned the top button of his white dress shirt.

Aimee Mikkelson seemed to be exactly who she claimed to be. He was glad about that. Tomorrow he wouldn't spend one moment worrying over her.

He hung his suit coat in his closet and went to the kitchen

for a bottle of cranberry juice. He cracked it open and took a long swig. Nope, he wouldn't spend one more minute thinking about the cute blond with more words than Chef Tony had complaints.

The next day, Dillon stared down the hall at Aimee talking to one of the maids. Aimee wore a purple filmy dress that reminded him of a fairy or flower petals. The maid opened a room door, and Aimee disappeared inside. He'd seen Aimee enter the hotel and even greeted her without a second thought. But now what was she up to?

He strode down the hall to the maid standing next to her service cart. "Brigitte, who just entered that room?"

Brigitte turned quickly and sucked in a breath. "Oh, sir, you startled me." Her heavy French accent slurred the words together. "I did not ask the lady her name. She said she did not have her key and would I please open the door for her."

Of course she didn't have a key. "Thank you, Brigitte."

"I hope I did not do anything wrong."

She really shouldn't have let Aimee in, but there was probably no harm done. "Next time a guest asks to be let into a room, send them to the front desk."

"Oui."

Dillon glanced at the room number, then headed back to the front desk and typed the room number into the computer system. She could simply be visiting with a guest of the hotel.

Or not.

The room came up as vacant. He grabbed the room key and strode back down the hall.

When he opened the door, he didn't see Aimee. He walked around and saw tiny white feet with a pair of purple sandals on them protruding from the closet. The body they were attached to was on hands and knees inside. "What are you doing?"

She froze, then swung her head and looked over her shoulder. "Hi, Dillon."

Hi, Dillon? "What are you doing in the closet?"

"I lost a contact." She swung her head back into the closet.

He swiped a hand down his face. She was kidding, right? "Please come out of the closet."

"Found it!" She backed out and stood up with her index finger extended. Resting on the end of her finger sat a hard contact lens. "I'm just going to run into the bathroom and pop this back in." She walked away.

He stood stationary. So she really had lost a contact. But that didn't explain what she was doing in this room to begin with. He heard the water run, and a moment later Aimee reappeared.

Aimee blinked rapidly as she approached him. "I just hate it when that happens. But it's back in now."

"How did you lose a contact *in the closet?*"

"I guess it just popped out. I need to be going." She headed for the door.

He just bet she did. "Wait."

She turned back to him with a smile. "What do you need?"

"I need to know what you are doing in this room. You told me yesterday you didn't have a room at this hotel."

She slumped her shoulders and cocked her head to one side. "It's like this. I figure I'm not going to have a chance to see this beautiful hotel that I have heard so many wonderful things about. It is absolutely fabulous. I have never seen a finer one. See, I could never afford to stay in a place this nice and just wanted a peek at one of the rooms. I promise I didn't hurt anything."

"Why didn't you just ask one of the wedding guests who does have a room here to show you their room?"

She raised a hand and waved it in the air. "Everyone is so busy with the wedding, and those who aren't are around touring the island. I didn't see any harm in a little peek. You can look around and see that I didn't disturb anything."

He took a deep breath. The room seemed fine. "Come with me." He led her to the front desk. He typed in the Presidential Suite, and as he thought, it, too, came up vacant. The nicest room in the hotel. She would enjoy seeing it. He grabbed the key. "Follow me."

Her eyes widened. "Where are you taking me?"

"I want to show you something." Why was he even doing this? Because she would appreciate the view? Maybe she wouldn't feel the need to roam around the building? He let her enter the elevator first and then pressed the appropriate button.

She stood across the elevator from him. "I really didn't hurt anything."

"I know." He gave her a smile to reassure her.

"That maid isn't going to get into any trouble, is she? She really thought she was helping someone. Well, she was. She was helping me get a small glimpse of how the other half lives."

"I've spoken to her." The elevator dinged, and the doors opened. None too soon. This girl could talk Chef Tony quiet. "This way." He pointed down the hall.

"Are you planning on throwing me off the turret?"

He couldn't help but laugh at that. "This hotel doesn't have a turret."

She raised her eyebrows. "The roof then."

He shook his head. "You have quite an imagination. A body landing in front of the hotel would not be good for business." He stopped in front of a set of double doors and unlocked them. "You wanted to see what one of our rooms looked like. This is one of our finest."

&

Aimee stared at the open doors, then back at Dillon. Was he trying to impress her with a fancy room? "You have been really nice and all, but I don't go to hotel rooms with guys." At least she had thought he was nice. But maybe all his attention yesterday wasn't him being helpful. Maybe he had ill-conceived intentions. She had seen the door to the stairs, and she knew, if he decided to push his advantage, how to grind the heel of her shoe into his foot to cause enough pain to get away.

He held up his hands and took a step backward. "This is nothing like that. I was merely allowing you to tour one of the rooms."

She squinted at him.

He stood in the open doorway. "My only intention is to give you the opportunity to see one of our luxury suites. Take it or leave it."

She gave him a sideways glance as she stepped inside. This was very nice of him. Guilt twisted inside her. "Thank you for doing this."

She turned her attention to the room and sucked in a long breath. This was a side of life she never dreamed of seeing, let alone live. She took in everything from the antique furnishings to the fresh flowers. She opened a door off to the right, a grand master bedroom. Another bedroom was off to the left. Each bedroom had its own bathroom and a powder room was situated near the living room. "My whole apartment could fit in just one of these rooms."

He remained stationed by the open doors. "Mine, too."

"This is gorgeous. I never realized a hotel room could be so grand in every way, the lavish furnishings and spaciousness. . . People really live like this?"

"Some do." He walked over to a pair of glass doors and swung them open. "Check out the view."

She stepped out onto the balcony and, with a sigh, took in the beautiful panorama of the Mackinac Bridge.

She exited the room with Dillon. "Thank you for letting me see that gorgeous view."

Dillon pulled the doors closed. "You liked it?"

"Of course." Her guilt wrenched tighter. Here he was being nice, and she had been trying to be sneaky. *I know, Lord, honesty is the best policy. I promise, no more lies. I'm really trying. Honest.* It wasn't as if she made a habit of lying. It was as though she had a short in her brain or something since stepping foot on Mackinac Island. Her need to find Nonie's treasure seemed to be driving her tongue.

Later that night, back in her room, she phoned the nursing home again. It had been a challenge to talk Dillon out of escorting her to the rehearsal dinner for the wedding she wasn't even a part of. It had been hard for her not to trip over him after he'd caught her in the hallway trying to figure out how to get inside that room a second time. She knew she could find what she was looking for if she just had the chance to search. She hadn't had enough time the first time. Now she only had tomorrow.

Betty picked up the phone at the nurses' station again. "Hi, Betty. Is Nonie still awake?"

"She is refusing to take her meds until you call, and she has the phone huddled next to her in bed. I'll connect you to her room."

"Thanks." Then she heard a click and a ring.

"Is that you, Muffin?"

The eagerness in her grandma's words warmed her heart. "Yes, Nonie. I hear you're giving the doctors and nurses a little trouble."

"People think they can run over you when you're blind. They talk about you like you were deaf and couldn't hear a word."

"Nonie, promise me you'll take your medication."

"Oh, the doctors just like to fuss. I'm not really in much pain." Her voice had the weak rasp of a worn-out elderly person. "If I took pills every time I had a little ache or pain, I'd be too full to eat a proper meal. You know, they have a pill for everything these days, and not a one will cure a thing."

Aimee closed her eyes and schooled her frustration. "Promise you'll do what the doctors say."

"Even if they don't know anything?"

"Nonie." Her grandma's stubbornness and tenacity were encouraging.

A heavy sigh came over the line. "Fine, I'll behave."

"And take your medication."

"Of course, of course." She could picture Nonie waving her hand as if batting at a fly as she said it. "Now tell me about the hotel. I wish I could have seen it just once. Is it as grand as its name?"

"Even more so. I wish you were with me now. When you get better, I'll bring you here. It's beautiful."

Nonie's voice took on a soft, wistful tone. "You are the only one who ever really believed, you know? Everyone just thinks I'm a crazy old woman trying to make up for her lack of vision. I'm not even going to ask you about *it*. I'm content that you believe enough to even go look."

She had to smile. By simply mentioning *it*, Nonie *was* asking and expecting an answer. "It's been a little harder than I expected." If Dillon would leave her alone, it would be a snap.

"That's all right, muffin. These things take time."

But she was almost out of time. She would need to check out of this room tomorrow. And if she couldn't slip past the watchful eye of Dillon Thurough, she wasn't going to have any more success tomorrow.

"What Granddad left may not even still be there. Someone else could have found it years ago. As I said, it is enough that you truly believe."

Nonie's words were brave, but Aimee knew deep down her grandma really wanted the treasure to be found. Exactly why, she wasn't sure. Nonie was always worried about medical expenses. Aimee was sure that was the driving force behind Nonie's talk of dying. She didn't want to be a burden to her loved ones any longer. Nonie probably wanted the treasure to help pay for her medical bills, as well, but would it even be anything of value to anyone outside the family? Outside her and Nonie?

Aimee had to admit that the nursing home was expensive. Nonie's Social Security and Medicare didn't cover everything, and coming up with the additional money was a challenge at times.

"You take as much time as you need, muffin."

See, there it was in her voice, as well as her words. It really did matter to Nonie if the treasure was found. Just believing wasn't all she wanted. The problem was, she couldn't take as much time as she needed. Time was her enemy. . .and Dillon Thurough. "You obey the doctors, or I'm coming home right this instant."

"I will."

"I love you, Nonie."

"I love you, too, muffin."

Aimee hung up the phone. How much did it cost to make

long-distance calls from a hotel room? She called the front desk and requested the amount. She didn't want to be surprised in the morning.

What she needed was a plan. A plan for how she could avoid Dillon, find what she came for, and get it out of the hotel without anyone seeing her. And if Dillon did see her, she would have to go to the wedding because he would likely dog her until she arrived safely and was seated. But if she could keep out of Dillon's sight, then the wedding would be the perfect opportunity to search. A lot of the staff, including Dillon, would be occupied with the event. Or maybe if the Lord were willing, Dillon would have the day off. It would be Sunday, after all. The hotel couldn't work him all the time. And since it would be Sunday, she would start the day off with church. That little stone church near the hotel would be great; then she wouldn't be far from her destination. And she could ask the Lord to keep Dillon occupied.

three

Dillon rolled over in bed, punched his pillow down for the tenth time, and dropped his head back onto it. The clock read 2:43. He needed sleep. He closed his eyes and took a deep breath. Aimee's smiling face drifted through his thoughts. He could picture her going in and out of every room. This was no use. He sat up and swung his legs over the side of the bed, raking his hands through his hair. She was not roaming around the hotel. He had to make himself believe that. He still couldn't convince his brain to accept the fact.

He dressed and headed over to the hotel. If he could just see with his own eyes that she wasn't snooping around, then maybe he could sleep. He just had this feeling she was up to something, but she hadn't done anything that he would really call wrong. Still, his gut told him there was something more to Aimee than met the eye.

He walked the hotel from top to bottom. He strolled down the hall he'd found her in several times and filled his lungs with a cleansing breath. She wasn't here. Once back in the lobby, his insides jumped. A blond stood, waiting for the elevator and leaning on a man's arm. *Aimee?*

He strode toward the elevator and reached it as the couple stepped onto it and turned. He sucked in a quick breath. It wasn't her.

The man held his hand on the door. "You going up?"

Dillon shook his head and let the door close. He had finally lost it. He was chasing shadows at three in the morning.

She's not here. Go home.

Lord, help me forget about her and sleep.

He finally fell asleep around four.

He rolled over and pried one eye open, then sprang out of bed an hour late. How could he have slept through his alarm? Church was just about to begin. He took a two-minute shower, popped in his contacts, and chugged a small bottle of cranberry juice on his walk to the church. He'd be late, but not so late as to miss the entire service. And he needed to be in the Lord's house this morning more than ever, to prepare himself for the day ahead—a day of keeping one eye on Aimee and the other on taking care of all the arrangements for the wedding and reception to follow. He needed this small respite that church provided before. . .Aimee.

Today would be challenging enough with the wedding arrangements without throwing in the suspicious Aimee and very little sleep. He would make it through on one prayer at a time. *Lord, help me to focus on You and not on how I'm going to locate Aimee once I get to the hotel. You know where she is. Please keep her out of trouble.*

He sat in the last pew just in time to bow his head for the opening prayer after the singing. He always enjoyed the singing, but he hadn't missed the meat of the service. He stared at the woman's wavy blond hair in front of him. It was oddly familiar.

Aimee.

He smiled to himself. Well, at least now he could focus on the sermon and not wonder what she was up to. *Thank You, Lord.* She was in church on her vacation, which had to say something positive about her character.

❧

After the closing prayer, Aimee stood up from the pew. The service had been very nice. She sent up a thankful prayer to the Lord. It had been just what she needed to clear her head of worry.

"Aimee?"

She rolled her eyes and tried not to sigh audibly at the sound of Dillon's voice. She would shake him loose from her, even if she had to be rude to do it. She spun with a smile to face him. Her pink floral lace dress swished around her ankles. "Dillon."

"Fancy seeing you here."

Had he followed her here to keep an eye on her?

He smiled, and his dimples pulled into his cheeks.

How could she be rude to him with those cute dimples? "I don't like to miss a Sunday."

"Me neither."

"Good morning, Dillon."

Dillon turned to an elderly woman in her sixties with her silver white hair combed away from her face and curled under, just below her ears. "Good morning to you, too, Mrs. Mayhew. As always, you look beautiful." Next to the woman stood Henry, the doorman from the hotel.

"Thank you." She tipped her head, then turned to Aimee. "You must introduce me to your young lady." The woman held her hand out to her.

Aimee shook her hand. "Aimee Mikkelson. I'm not his young lady. We just ran into each other here."

"I'm Constance Mayhew."

"Nice to meet you." She turned to Henry. "And good morning to you, Henry."

"The pleasure is mine, Miss Mikkelson."

"Oh, please call me Aimee."

Constance gave her an indulging smile, then turned back to Dillon. "I was concerned when you weren't in the service on time. I was afraid you might have come down with something, the way you work so hard."

Well, that ruled out him following her. He obviously attended this church regularly. Just her misfortune to choose his church. But it was nice to know he was dedicated.

Dillon held a worn study Bible in one hand. "No need to worry. I merely overslept."

"Because you work too hard."

This seemed like a good time to leave. "I'm going to head out. It was nice meeting you, Constance. Henry, I'll probably see you at the hotel."

"I have Sundays and Wednesdays off, so I won't be at the hotel today."

"Well, bye then." She picked up her purse, but before she could pick up her camera bag, Dillon slung the bag's strap over his shoulder. "I'll walk with you." He escorted her out and toward the hotel.

Why did he have to be so nice? The guilt twisted tighter. *Yes, Lord, I could tell him the truth, but it's just so much harder now.* Maybe she could do something nice for him in return. *But what? Any suggestions, Lord?*

They reached the hotel entrance, and a young carrottopped doorman opened the door. She had seen him working as a bell-hop yesterday.

"Thank you, Kevin." Dillon stepped aside for her to enter first.

She nodded to Kevin. "Thank you."

"Oh, Mr. Thurough," Kevin said. "One of the mothers from the wedding party was looking for you. She seemed really frazzled."

Aimee grimaced. That sounded like trouble.

"Excuse me." Dillon handed her the camera bag and strode across the lobby to a large middle-aged woman in a mint green beaded dress standing at the front desk.

Here was her chance to lose Dillon for the day. But something drew her toward the turmoil in which Dillon was trapped.

As she approached, Dillon was holding his hands out as if to pat down the woman's anxiety. "What exactly is the problem, Mrs. Whitehall?"

"Madison's cousin Sherry was going to do Madison's hair. She does it up in this twist that is so flattering on Madison. But, three days before the wedding, Sherry goes rollerblading with her children and breaks one wrist and sprains the other. I didn't even make the connection until yesterday that she couldn't do Maddy's hair. What was she doing skating so close to the wedding?"

Aimee watched Dillon's face pinch together. He seemed to be having a hard time following her. "We sent up a hairdresser to take care of the problem."

Mrs. Whitehall continued, "Who didn't speak a lick of English."

"She's supposed to be very good."

Mrs. Whitehall was quite distressed. "But she can't understand what we want and was doing something entirely different. I sent her away."

Dillon took a deep breath. "There is no need for alarm. I'll call the salon and have another hairstylist sent up."

Mrs. Whitehall took a deep breath. "Thank you."

"Wait here, and I'll make the call." Dillon walked over to the front desk and picked up the phone.

Dillon was good at his job. He didn't panic or get upset or tell Mrs. Whitehall she was freaking out over nothing. He patiently listened to her dilemma and set out to solve it calmly.

Dillon hung up the phone and came back. "Mrs. Whitehall, Carole will be up to your suite in ten minutes."

"She speaks English?"

"As well as you or I."

Mrs. Whitehall let out a heavy sigh. "Thank you." Then she glanced at Aimee and back to Dillon. "Is this your other photographer? Maddy is so happy she's taking additional pictures. Is she available to come up to our suite to take before and after shots?"

Aimee sucked in a soft, quick breath. *Oops.* Mrs. Whitehall was asking the wrong person, so she chimed in before Dillon could respond. "I'd be happy to."

Mrs. Whitehall smiled. "We're in the Jacqueline Kennedy Suite."

"I'll come with you now, if that's all right?" It was probably best if she didn't hang around for Dillon to ask questions. Besides, she had said she would take pictures and that she would make good on her fib, so now she must atone for her sin. She had no one to blame but herself for her troubles.

She followed Mrs. Whitehall into the suite and onto the navy blue carpet with gold Presidential eagles woven into it. This room was decorated differently from the other two she'd been in, but it did remind her of the first lady it was named after—classy and regal.

"Maddy, we have a new stylist coming up. . .and look who I found."

Maddy disengaged herself from the fray of women, skipped across the room, and hugged Aimee, then introduced the bridesmaids, Kathy, Debbie, Jessi, Laura, Anna, and the matron-of-honor Genie, short for Eugenia. Each of them was armed with a disposable camera. "Take pictures of everything," Maddy said with a wave of her arm.

"But it looks like everyone here has a camera. What do you need me for?"

"No one person can be everywhere. You will see things

no one else does. I want oodles of pictures to choose from. Besides, you're a professional."

How did she figure that? "I wouldn't call myself a professional." She did like to take pictures though. "What about the groom? Won't you be short on pictures of him?"

"I gave my brother ten cameras. Those guys better be taking pictures."

Who was she to argue with the bride? She snapped pictures of the friends interacting and teasing each other. And later, when they all would leave for the ceremony, Aimee would hang back at the hotel. Carole managed to arrange Maddy's hair in a way she liked, even with four people giving her different instructions.

When the bridesmaids prepared to leave to ride in the first coach, Aimee said, "I'll take off now, too."

Maddy grabbed her arm. "You can't. I need you to take a picture of Mom putting on my veil and me getting into the carriage. And getting out of the carriage."

This girl wanted every minute of the day recorded on film. "Won't the other photographer be taking those pictures?" And it might be best if Aimee left before he arrived.

"He's already at the church getting shots of my Huey and the other guys."

"Then I can snap a few pictures of your mom pinning on your veil and you getting into the carriage. But I'm sure the other photographer will get several of you stepping out of the carriage."

"Yes, I'm sure he will. And you can ride with us and take pictures in the carriage."

She tried to back out, but Maddy refused to take no for an answer. Aimee refrained from sighing audibly and resigned herself to no other choice but to attend the wedding of strangers.

Aimee sat in the back of the church and watched Madison Whitehall and Huey Dodson exchange marriage vows. It was a nice wedding, even if she didn't know anybody. This was where lying had gotten her. She was now occupied during the only time she had to search for Nonie's inheritance—because of her lie. The very thing that had enabled her to get inside the hotel was keeping her from searching.

Thou shalt not lie.

She glanced heavenward. *I've learned my lesson.*

four

Late that evening, Dillon breathed a sigh of relief as he watched Aimee walk to the end of the porch and onto Cadotte Avenue. Another day survived. It had been a challenge to keep an eye on her and see that everything went smoothly for the Dodson-Whitehall reception.

Aimee was almost out of sight when he remembered he had wanted to ask her if she was returning tomorrow. It wasn't anything personal; he just wanted to be prepared. Not that there was really any way to prepare for Aimee. She just sort of happened—like a hurricane.

He hurriedly followed her. She cut back onto the hotel grounds. What was she doing? And why was she going this way? He followed her along the path in the thick trees between the hotel and the south shore of the island, past the bike shack; then she headed away from the hotel. She stepped several paces off the path and crouched down.

At first, he couldn't see what she was doing, but he was sure he heard a thick zipper; then he saw what looked like a suitcase lid flipped open. What was she doing? He stepped closer until he was at the edge of the path. Any closer and he'd be crunching dead undergrowth and give away his presence. Another zipper and lid. He could see now that she was crouched in front of two suitcases.

She shouldn't be here at this time of night. "What are you doing?"

She stood, spinning around to face him, and the skirt of her pink lacy dress swished around her. Her eyes rounded. Then she smiled. "Isn't this a nice surprise?"

Surprise? Yes. Nice? He doubted it.

She stepped sideways, putting herself between him and a view of her suitcases. "What brings you out here?"

"You. Are you staying out here?" He made a sweeping motion with his hand to encompass the wooded area.

She stepped toward him. "Can we talk about this?"

"I thought you had a room at one of the other lodging establishments on the island. You implied you did. Have you been sleeping out here?"

Her expression turned sheepish. "I had a room up until this morning, and then I had to check out. I'm just not ready to leave this wonderful place. I want to stay a couple more days."

"Out here?" He glanced at the surrounding trees. "Why don't you book another room?"

"Why, when this is so gorgeous? I don't want to be cooped up in a little room." She drank in a deep breath. "Just smell that fresh air. I know I'll sleep good here tonight."

Sleep out here? The logic of a female mind. "You can't sleep here."

"Why not? I'm not hurting anything."

"You just can't. It's illegal. You can't camp on the hotel grounds or anywhere else on the island." He pointed to her suitcases. "Close up your luggage, and I'll find you a room at the hotel."

She bit her bottom lip and looked to the ground. "I can't exactly afford a room at the Grand Hotel."

He could barely hear her. "Then I'll find you something in town you can afford."

She locked her baby blue gaze on him and spread her hands out. "This is all I can afford. I promise I won't be any trouble to anyone. Please let me stay." She flashed that smile of hers. "Please."

He scrubbed his face with his hands. This couldn't be happening. She had nowhere to go, but she couldn't stay here. He could suggest she leave the island then. She would probably agree and make it look as though she were leaving, only to find some other place to camp out. "Get your luggage. I'll think of something."

She closed her suitcases. He took them from her and carried them by the side handles.

She picked up her white purse and camera bag and stepped out onto the path. "You aren't going to turn me into the police or something, are you?"

Maybe that was the wisest thing to do. "On what charge?"

"I don't know. Trespassing or something?"

"I'll find you a place to stay for tonight, but you absolutely have to leave the island tomorrow if you can't afford to book yourself a room. Promise me that."

"Leave the island? But what if I'm not ready to leave?"

"Then rent yourself a room."

"Is there anyone on the island who would give me a room for free for a couple of nights?"

Other than him, a big pushover? "Not that I know of."

"Those have wheels you know." She pointed to her luggage. "It's much easier to roll them behind you."

"The dirt and debris on the forest floor would ruin the bearings in the wheels."

"That is so thoughtful of you. I didn't think of that when I rolled them out here."

He flashed back to the first time he saw her, two days ago, and his initial thought about her—trouble. She wasn't serious trouble for him. More of an inconvenience. And she hadn't caused any fuss for either the bride or groom. They seemed to like her, but something Mrs. Whitehall said stuck with him. *Is this your other photographer?* He hadn't thought about it at the time, but although Mrs. Whitehall had directed the comment to him, Aimee had swept her away. And what about her sneaking into one of the rooms and seeming to be frustrated with him for seeing that she arrived at the proper events? Then it hit him like a revelation. "You weren't really part of the wedding party, were you?"

"You saw me taking pictures with my digital camera. Some of the shots turned out great. I hope Maddy and Huey like them. They are such a darling couple. I'm praying that they have a long, happy marriage."

And she was trying to distract him with a subtle change in subject. *Not going to work, missy.* "But you don't *know* them?"

"Like *know* know or acquaintance know?"

He would make the question so direct she couldn't sidestep it. "Had you ever met either the bride or groom before you stepped foot on this island?"

She hesitated, then said, "No."

That was the shortest answer he had ever heard from her.

Then she continued, "But they were really nice when I met them. I got Huey's e-mail address, and I'm going to send him all the pictures, so I really did do what I said I was going to do."

He supposed she wouldn't be satisfied with a one-word answer for long without adding an addendum.

Once they reached the sidewalk, he set the suitcases on the cement and pulled up the extension handles to roll them. As he grabbed the second handle, so did Aimee. Her soft hand brushed against his. He remembered how it felt to hold it as he shook her hand the other day when they met.

She cocked her head to one side. "I can take one."

"I've got them."

"How chivalrous. This is all very nice of you."

Would she still think so when he questioned her as to her reason for being here. If he didn't like her answers or didn't believe them, he might still call the sheriff.

"There has been something lost in our country when guys don't carry a girl's books or open doors for ladies anymore, and things like that," Aimee said. "I'm not saying it is the fault of men or anything. They are just protecting themselves from crabby women who are offended by common courtesy. How could it be insulting for one person to hold a door open for another? I just don't see it. But here at your hotel, courtesy is paramount. People are always around to help in any way they can."

"We pride ourselves on service." He hoisted the suitcases up as he climbed the hotel's porch steps, then walked half the length of the porch to the front door.

The night doorman, Marvin, opened the door for them. "Good evening, sir."

"Thank you, Marvin." He let Aimee enter ahead of him.

"See, there it is again. Marvin opened the door, and you let me go in first. I'm just not used to it. Don't get me wrong. I like it. I'm just not used to it."

He set her luggage inside his office and motioned toward a burgundy leather chair opposite the desk. "Have a seat." He walked around and sat behind his oak desk. He folded his hands and rested them on the clean desk pad. "Ms. Mikkelson—"

"Please, call me Aimee." She shifted in her chair like a fidgety child.

"*Ms. Mikkelson*, since we have previously determined that you did not come for the wedding, please enlighten me on your purpose for being here."

"I thought you were finding me a place to stay."

"First, we must settle this matter."

She looked as though she might leap from the chair and bolt. Then he really would need to call the sheriff.

She looked at a picture on the wall, then glanced at his filing cabinet. Suddenly she developed an interest in her nails. "You see, it's like this: My great-great-grandfather helped build this hotel."

He closed his eyes and shook his head slightly. Was she for real? Did she really expect him to believe that?

"No, really. His name was Adam Wright. He was on one of the crews building this great hotel. If there is some record of who worked on the crews, you'll find his name right there. He met the daughter of one of the crew leaders and fell in love with her. Long story short, they got married and lived happily ever after. But Great-Great-Grandfather Adam told my great-great-grandmother that he left a secret buried inside this hotel for their future grandchildren to find—well, that was even before she consented to see him—but how could she say no to him when he was Mr. Wright?"

Cute joke, but he refused to acknowledge it. It would only encourage her.

She twisted one hand in the other. "Well, my grandma is the only living grandchild remaining, and she couldn't come because she's blind and fell and broke her hip, so I came to find it for her. I had to. She keeps talking about not living much longer. I wanted to make this dream happen for her before she dies, or maybe it will help pull her through so she'll get better. I just have to find what was left for her."

Her story was so fantastical and unreal. How could anyone make it up? He actually believed her. It wasn't the story, but the earnestness in her voice as she told it. He wanted to believe her. He couldn't believe he was about to ask this. "Just what did your great-grandfather leave here?"

"Great-great-grandfather."

"Fine. What did he supposedly leave behind?"

"I don't know. He never told Nonie. Just that she was to find it. He left her a riddle to help her. When she was old enough to figure out the riddle, she was old enough to appreciate the gift. She's ninety-three. I think she's old enough."

That was beside the point. "I don't suppose it would do any good to try to convince you that *if* your great-*great*-grandfather did work on the construction of this hotel that it was likely just a tale he told your grandmother, and he really didn't leave anything in these walls."

"Actually it's in the floor. The riddle says, 'In the wood below.' That has to be a wood floor."

"If there was something, it would have been discovered years ago. I'm sure it is no longer here."

Her mouth pulled down in a slight pout. "But I won't know if I don't at least look."

She definitely had a one-track mind. "And what do you plan to do with this *treasure* if you find it?"

"Take it back to Nonie, of course."

"Do you realize that removing items from the hotel would be considered stealing?"

She pinched her eyebrows together. "But it was left for her."

"But if it has been here since the hotel's construction, then it would be considered hotel property."

She stared at him without a word. He waited for her to assent that he was right and her quest futile.

She blinked several times. "Wow."

Did "wow" mean she understood?

She slapped her hand to her forehead. "Wow." She stood and walked out.

His office door hung open. It was his turn to stare. He turned his gaze to her suitcases, camera bag, and purse. She would be back in a moment. She had to.

After ten minutes, he checked his watch again. She couldn't go far without her things, and the last ferry had left for the night. He would give her a few more minutes.

When she hadn't returned in fifteen minutes, he left his office to locate her. Was she still in the hotel? Or had she left the grounds? He stopped at the front doors. "Marvin, did a young blond woman exit through these doors?"

"No, sir. But there is a pretty girl down there." Marvin pointed to the west end of the lobby.

Aimee stood at the windows looking out as she had the first day she arrived. He came up behind her. She must have sensed him there because she spoke. "It's beautiful."

He looked out into the darkness at the lighted Mackinac Bridge. He wasn't sure what else to say in that moment so dropped a piece of trivia. "The bridge is five miles long."

After a minute, she turned to face him. "You know that saying, 'Look before you leap?' Well, I don't. Look, that is. I see what needs to be done and just leap. No thought about how or the details. I work that stuff out as I go. Just go and do. You don't talk about painting a room; you just do it. If you don't like the color, paint over it. Someone else would study paint chips and research what color would be best."

Is this supposed to make sense?

"It may take them a month to decide, but they would pick out the right color the first time. I can have the room painted three or four times. But after a month, both rooms would be painted the right color. Does that make one way right and the other wrong?"

He couldn't even begin to comprehend the relevance. "What does that have to do with the current situation?"

"I just can't sit around and do nothing. I need to be active. You're right. Whatever Adam Wright left here belongs to the hotel. But where does that leave Nonie?"

He hoped that was a rhetorical question.

"I don't know what to do now."

"Let's go back to my office and get you a place to stay for the night."

She followed him with her shoulders slumped and her smile gone.

It was late and finding her lodging could take a little doing, especially when all she could afford was free. He brought up the hotel registry on his computer. He had the authorization to comp a room, but then he would need to report the room use and why to his boss. Rumors would start flying around the hotel. He didn't want to mess with any of that. The easiest solution was often the best. He would put her in his apartment and crash at Steve's. Steve would keep this to himself.

He took her suitcases and led her out of his office. "Follow me." He led her out the back of the hotel and across a narrow road to the hotel's staff apartment building. The accommodations were small but adequate. He unlocked his door for her.

"Is this your place?"

"Yes. Have a seat."

She remained by the door. "I can't stay here with you."

"Good, because you'll be staying here without me. I'm going to stay at Steve's for the night. You wanted free. This is free. It's the only offer you are going to get."

He went to his bedroom and packed an overnight bag and laid a suit bag with a fresh suit in it out on his bed. He went to the bathroom to pack his shaving kit and put that in his overnight bag. He returned to his small living area and set down his bag and suit.

Aimee stood by a shelf unit that held his book collection, as well as family photographs. It was the photos that seemed to hold her interest: his parents' wedding picture, his first fish with his dad... His gaze locked on the silver frame with his mom holding him as a baby. *Don't dwell.*

"Housekeeping put fresh sheets on today. I'll come back in the morning."

"This is really, really nice of you to give up your place for me."

Would she think him so nice when he escorted her to the ferry first thing in the morning? "It's only one night. And you will either find other accommodations or leave the island. Understood?"

She gulped and nodded.

❧

Dillon knocked on Steve's door, not looking forward to explaining why he needed a place to stay for the night.

Steve opened the door in boxers and a T-shirt and, after surveying the suit bag and overnight bag, said, "What's up?" but stepped aside to let him enter.

"Can I crash on your couch for the night?" He laid his suit bag over a wingback chair and his other bag on the floor.

"What's wrong with your place?"

"It's occupied."

"Bummer. By whom?"

He didn't want to answer that but did. "Aimee Mikkelson."

Steve's eyes widened. "That cute little blond who's been hanging around you the last couple of days?"

"She hasn't been hanging around me. I've been keeping an eye on her. And yes, she's the one."

"Buddy, am I to understand you right? You have a gorgeous babe in your apartment, and you are sleeping here?"

"There is nothing between us and never will be."

Steve's mouth pulled into a smile. "Then why don't you sleep on your own couch?"

"It's better this way."

"Because you're attracted to her."

"I don't have time to be attracted to Aimee or any other woman."

"Ah yes, your plan to become general manager of the Grand Hotel by age thirty-five."

He'd promised his mother as she lay dying that he'd buy her the Grand Hotel if she would only live. And when she died, he was still determined to buy it for her. But his seven-year-old mind didn't understand how impossible that would be. So, as he grew up, he settled for running the hotel his mother had always dreamed of visiting.

"Are the sacrifices worth it?"

Steve's question brought him out of his reverie. Dillon didn't think that Steve really wanted an answer to his rhetorical question, so he let it slide.

Steve retrieved the spare bedding from the top of the coat closet. Dillon had a similar set in his closet. Standard issue for the hotel's apartments.

"So if you really aren't interested in Aimee, you wouldn't mind if I showed her a little interest?"

What did it matter? She would be gone tomorrow. If she couldn't afford a room tonight, then she wouldn't be able to tomorrow either. "That's up to you."

"Sweet." Steve plopped the bedding onto the couch. "You'll have to make it up yourself."

"Thanks."

Steve gave him a wave as he headed to his bedroom.

Dillon pulled out his toiletry kit and headed for the bathroom. He dug through his bag but couldn't find the case for his contact lenses. He checked his pants pocket and his overnight bag. He couldn't wash up without removing his contacts. He headed back to his place and knocked on the door. There was no answer. He knocked louder. *Come on, Aimee. Answer the door.*

❧

Aimee walked out into Dillon's living room wearing the sweatshirt and sweatpants she used as pajamas, towel-drying her hair. The shower had felt more glorious than she'd thought possible. Maybe it was due to the fact she didn't know when she'd get to take an actual shower again while trying to evade Dillon and search the hotel. The task would be hard, but not impossible. She had to find the treasure tomorrow and then arrange to borrow what she found to show Nonie.

She stopped short when she saw Dillon sitting in an overstuffed chair on the far side of the room. "Dillon." She was glad he couldn't read her mind.

He stayed seated in the chair. "I forgot my contact lens case. You mind if I get it?"

"Don't you just hate it when you forget your case or lose it? I lost my case once when I was in college; well, I lost it more than once, but that's beside the point. Anyway, I took two glasses and put one contact in each with a little water and put them on opposite sides of the sink so I wouldn't put the left contact in my right eye and the right one in the left. The world looks funny when you do that. Have you ever done that?"

He shook his head. "I can't say that I have."

"Wow. I thought everyone had done that at least once." She shrugged. "So, in the morning, one of my contacts is gone and the glass empty. I asked my roommate if she knew what happened to it. Her eyes got real big and her face paled a bit, then she said, 'I dreamed I was in the desert and this fish came along and gave me some water.' I laughed so hard. You see my roommate walked in her sleep all the time. She drank my contact lens in her dream. I went around the entire day squinting with one eye so I could see halfway straight."

Dillon hadn't moved from the chair. He drew in a slow breath. "I'll just get my case. I have a full day tomorrow and need rest." He pushed out of the chair, then disappeared down the hall and returned a moment later holding up his lens case as if proof of his just intentions.

"I noticed you only have two DVDs. Is that really all you have?"

"I don't have much extra time to indulge in television."

"Then Constance was right. You work too much."

"I do what needs to be done."

She plucked the DVDs off his shelf. "I haven't heard of either one of these movies."

"Both of those movies were filmed at this hotel. The hotel pool was built for Esther Williams for her 1947 movie, *This Time for Keeps*. The movie *Somewhere in Time* came out in 1980."

"Let me guess. You only have these movies for research."

"As I said, I don't have a lot of extra time."

"You should make time. Which one do you recommend?" She held one up in each hand.

"It doesn't matter. They are both supposed to be good."

"Supposed? You mean you haven't watched them?"

"Not clear through. Just bits and pieces."

She held up the older one. "Let's watch this one."

"You can watch whichever one you want. I have work tomorrow." He turned and left.

She stared at the closed door. There was a guy who seriously needed to relax.

five

Dillon stepped out of Steve's bathroom the next morning to find a sleepy-eyed Steve approaching the door. Steve surveyed him in his charcoal suit. "I suppose you're all packed, too."

"I'll be out of your hair in thirty seconds. Thanks for letting me stay here." He dropped his shaving kit into his overnight bag and zipped it closed.

Steve's mouth stretched into a wide yawn. He shook it free. "We have a meeting with the big guy at eight, right?"

"Yes. See you there." He picked up his bags and headed out the door.

He knocked on his apartment door and waited, but Aimee didn't answer. She was probably sleeping late if she stayed up to watch one of the movies after he left. He would sneak in quietly, drop off his bags, and leave her a note to come find him.

When he entered, the place was quiet and dark, the bedroom door closed. He hung his suit bag from a floor lamp in the living room to keep his suit from getting wrinkles and set down his other bag. He pulled out a sheet of paper from the drawer by the phone. After penning his note to have her go to the front desk to have him paged, he left for his day's work.

As he crossed the lobby to head for his office, he stopped short and stared at Aimee talking to the assistant general manager. *Please, Lord, let her hold her tongue.*

Maybe he could defuse any brewing trouble. He approached them. "Mr. Howard, good morning."

Mr. Howard in a light gray suit and red tie had small squinty eyes on an almost symmetrically round head. He styled his thinning dark hair combed to one side. "Dillon, just the man I wanted to see."

He hoped it was for a good reason and not an "Aimee" reason.

Mr. Howard continued, "I've just hired this young lady to be your assistant for the Lilac Festival."

"You what?" Shouldn't that have been his own responsibility to choose an assistant?

"You were saying that you needed help?"

"Yes, I was." *But I didn't want you to hire a stowaway who wants to find buried treasure in the floor of the hotel.*

"Her name is Aimee Mikkelson."

"Ms. Mikkelson." He dipped his head toward her.

"Please call me Aimee." She gave him a frisky smile.

"Aimee, I assume you have references."

"Go ahead and check her references, but I've already hired her. She has some good ideas. Use her in whatever capacity you see fit." Mr. Howard turned to leave, then turned back. "And see that she's put on the payroll."

He wanted to grimace or growl—something to release his current frustration. "I'll take care of it, sir." Mr. Howard had no idea what he was getting the hotel in for. He also had no qualms about stepping on other people's toes.

Once Mr. Howard was out of earshot, Dillon turned to Aimee. "What do you think you are doing?"

"You said if I couldn't pay for a room then I'd have to leave the island. Now that I have a job, I can afford a room and I can stay. Isn't that wonderful?" Her smile stretched wider.

Wonderful wasn't the word he would have chosen. "What tale did you tell to wheedle a job out of him?"

"No tale. I told him I needed a job and no duty was beneath

me. I liked people, and I'd try any task put before me and wasn't afraid to ask for clarification or guidance if I didn't understand something."

The perfect employee? He refused to believe that. His initial thought that she'd be trouble for him was coming true.

Aimee continued in her bright cheery tone. "Then he asked me some questions about my background—which I answered very honestly. Oh, can I have an advance on my paycheck so I can rent a room? I understand it is not permissible to sleep outside."

He would not growl or grimace. He drew in a deep breath instead. "I need to get you on the payroll first, but before even that, I have a meeting to prepare for. Follow me." He walked back to his office and let her in first.

"What do you want me to do?"

He drew in a controlling breath and pointed to the chair she had occupied the night before. "Sit there and don't say a word." He went to his filing cabinet, pulled out several forms, and handed them to her. "Fill these out. I need the information to get you into the system."

He sat behind his desk and tried to figure out what to do with her. He pushed papers around and pulled out his notes for the meeting. What was he going to do with her? Should he tell Mr. Howard why she had come in the first place? That would surely get her fired before she even started. He had nothing against Aimee, but if she caused trouble and Mr. Howard found out that he knew and didn't report it, his job could be on the line. He couldn't and wouldn't risk his job for her. This job was more important than a pretty face. So far, she hadn't done anything that was really wrong. And he did feel sorry for her and her misguided intentions. He would just have to keep an eye on her and keep her so busy she didn't have time to be searching the hotel for a mythical treasure. If she seemed to be getting out of control or not doing the job she was hired to do, then he would take it to Mr. Howard.

"I can help you with that."

Aimee's soft voice tugged him out of his thoughts. He should have known she couldn't stay silent. "I have a meeting to attend."

"What do you want me to do while you're gone? I could roam around the hotel and get to know the layout."

Leave Aimee unsupervised? And free to roam? That didn't seem wise. He pulled a steno pad and pen from his desk and gave them to Aimee. "Come with me, don't say a word, and take notes. Do you think you can do that?"

She huffed out a breath. "I may be blond, but I'm not dumb."

His nerves might be a bit frayed, but he would not snap at her. *Lord, please guard my tongue.* "I never thought you were. My concern was whether or not you could remain quiet for that long."

She gifted him with a smile. "Oh. Of course I can."

"Good. Then do it."

She gave him a salute but didn't say a word.

❧

Aimee followed Dillon into the conference room, the first to arrive, and Dillon pulled out a chair for her at the long wooden table. "Thank you." Somehow it seemed to fit him that he would be the first one at a meeting.

Before Dillon could sit down, he greeted another man entering; then Dillon sat on one side of her and the other man, about Dillon's age, sat on her other side. "Aimee, this is Steve Newton, assistant manager."

She held out her hand. "Nice to meet you, Steve."

Steve took her hand in both of his and held it. "Believe me, the pleasure is all mine."

Steve was obviously a flirt. She smiled at him and retrieved her hand. "You are the one who let Dillon stay at your place last night."

"What can I say? I'm just a nice guy. If you ever need a place to stay, my door is always open."

"How sweet." But she suspected the offer wasn't the same one she'd received from Dillon last night. She turned to Dillon. "I thought you were the assistant manager here."

"I'm assistant manger over special events: weddings, Lilac Festival, and things like that. Steve is over amenities like the stables, bike shop, swimming pool, and the golf course."

"So who was Mr. Howard?"

"He's the assistant general manager."

"He's over all of us." Steve jumped in. "Which is the job our boy Dillon is vying for on his way to general manager."

"Wow. You are ambitious."

Several other well-dressed men and women had entered. Most of them mingled by the table with food and beverages at the end of the room.

Wow. This was like a real job. Not like clerking at the grocery store or a sales associate at the department store. Not having finished college, her employment opportunities had been limited. Maybe after her work here at the hotel was through, she could return to college and complete her education.

She stood up from the conference table. "Can I get either of you anything before the meeting starts?"

Dillon looked up at her. "You don't have to wait on me."

"Oh, I'm not. I'm going to get myself something and thought I could grab you something, as well. Just trying to be nice and all."

Dillon conceded. "I'll take cranberry juice."

She turned to Steve.

"Coffee, black."

She went to the table at the end of the room with fruit, muffins, bagels, and a variety of drinks on it. She took a glass—a real glass, not a plastic cup—and poured cranberry juice from the decanter. The juice looked good. She poured herself some.

Then she took a ceramic mug and filled it with coffee. She dropped in a sugar cube and poured in a dab of cream. After filling a plate with a blueberry muffin and some fruit, she balanced the plate on her forearm and held both glasses by their bottoms on one hand and grabbed Steve's coffee in the other.

As she set Steve's coffee in front of him, he said, "Impressive."

"Five years as a waitress."

She set the plate and glasses on the table and sat down. She noticed Steve looking into his cup.

She sucked in a breath. "Oh. I'm sorry. I put cream and sugar in it. That's how I like it. I wasn't thinking. I'll go get you some more."

As she started to stand, Steve put a hand on her arm. "It's fine. I like to live dangerously." He winked at her.

She would need to watch out for Steve. He was a charmer. Or at least was trying to be.

❧

After the meeting, back in Dillon's office, Dillon sat behind his desk. "Steve was hitting on you."

The dumb-blond thing again? "Like I couldn't tell. Oops. I'm sorry, that was rude. I should have just said, 'Yes, I know.' But sometimes when I open my mouth, things just jump out, and then I have to go back and try to fix them. I'll be quiet now." She folded her hands in her lap.

Dillon looked at her a moment before he spoke. "I wasn't

implying anything about your IQ. Just watch yourself around Steve."

"I know, and I am sorry. It's just that, for my whole life, guys and gals alike have treated me as though I'm an airhead. I got almost all straight As in high school and all As and Bs in the two years I went to college except for that one C; but that was because I missed the final because my sister was in the hospital, and I had to make it up. And you really don't care."

"Are you nervous around me?"

"Nervous around you? No, not that I can think of. Why?"

"I just thought that that might be the reason you talk a lot."

"No. I just like to talk."

"I can tell."

"Doesn't everyone like to talk?"

"Evidently some more than others."

She was the *some*, and he was one of the *others*. "Since we are on the subject of talking, do you always consider each word before you speak? Do you ever just say the first thing that comes to your mind?"

He hesitated a moment, then said, "Words are not something to be flung about like plastic necklaces at a Mardi Gras parade."

"I'll take that as a no."

He furrowed his brow, then moved some papers around on his desk. "You got an overview of the Lilac Festival in the meeting. It's an important nine-day event on the island."

"I got that. And I just wanted to assure you that I will do whatever duties you need me to do. I won't go off looking for my family treasure during work hours; I'll wait until after office hours. I won't disturb any guests or get in the way of any of the staff. I promise."

He just stared at her.

What was he thinking? Did he believe her? "I haven't known you long enough to be able to interpret that look, so words would be really useful right now."

He stood and came around his desk. "Come with me." He held the office door for her and led the way to the front desk. "I need a room key." After receiving the key, he led her down the west hall to the end. He inclined his chin toward the door. "Why is this room important to you? Or were you going to do a room-by-room search of the hotel?"

He was going to let her in the room? "My great-great-grandfather left a riddle, sort of a poem. 'In a grand hall, walk west to the wall, you tread to the treasure, a gift without measure. Then north you must turn, for the prize you will earn, at the closet, humble and low, a treasure in the wood below.' I figured that since the hotel doesn't have a room called the grand hall and the riddle says *a* and not *the* that it is referring to the hallway. And obviously this direction is west; north there is a room with a closet. Hence the reason I was crawling around in the closet."

"What if you find what you are looking for in there? Then what?"

"Then we take it back to your office?"

He slowly filled his lungs. "I mean, you can't take it from the hotel, so what good will it be to you?"

"Well. . .I thought we could tell the owners the whole story, and maybe they would let me borrow it to take to Nonie, then bring it back. I wish Nonie could keep it, but I know that is too much to hope for."

Seemingly satisfied with her answer, Dillon stepped forward and unlocked the door.

"I can't believe you are doing this," she said as she stepped inside.

Dillon followed her. "You'll be more productive if you aren't trying to figure out ways to get inside this room."

"I wish I had come to you in the first place, but by the time I thought of that, it was too late." She went straight for the closet.

He put a hand on her arm. "Here. Let me. You're in a dress." He knelt inside the closet. "Exactly what am I looking for in here?"

"I don't know. Maybe a loose board or something." She stretched up on her tiptoes to peer over him.

He pulled out a pocketknife and poked at the seams between the cedar boards. "These boards are all solid." He pulled at the baseboards, then backed out of the closet and stood.

She blinked the moisture back from her eyes. A tear tumbled down her cheek. She wiped it away.

He furrowed his brow. "What's wrong?"

She dried the tear with her palm. "This was possibly the nicest thing anyone has ever done for me."

"But I didn't find anything."

"But you were willing to try." Another tear escaped.

He went to the bathroom and brought back a tissue for her.

She dabbed at her eyes. She was being silly, crying like this. His actions had just hit her sentimental side.

"Let's go back to my office."

By the time they reached his office, she had pulled her errant emotions under control. Dillon resumed his position of authority behind his desk. She sat in the chair across from him.

He picked up a pen from his desk. "I need to know your intentions now."

She widened her eyes. "My intentions?"

"I didn't take you down to that room to help you *find* your treasure. I took you down there to show you there was no treasure. So now that you know whatever might have been there is gone, what do you intend to do about the job you took this morning?"

"When Mr. Howard hired me for the duration of the Lilac Festival, that was like a promise that I'd be here at least through the end of the festival. If you're asking if I'm going to leave now, I'm not. Even I know that sometimes I can be a little flighty and sporadic, but I won't let you down. I intend to stay. And besides, maybe after a few days of studying the riddle, I can figure out someplace else to look." *Oops.* Maybe she shouldn't have said that last part out loud. *Too late now.* He would feel a need to keep his eye on her every move, and that really wasn't necessary.

He took a deep breath. "Promise me you won't go roaming around the building looking in every available room."

"I'll do you one better. I promise to come to you with any new theories I come up with, and you can help me with them."

She wasn't sure he liked that idea, but he did nod.

"Don't you have a home and job you need to be getting back to?"

"You could say I'm at a crossroads in my life. I was guardian of my nephew for the past five years. Well, not really this last year because he's been at college." She would skip the part about her sister being mentally ill, which had forced Aimee into her temporary guardianship role. "I asked for time off from my boss, so I could come here. She said no because of the big sale coming up at the store, so I gave her my two-week notice. I couldn't keep my apartment on my waitress pay, even though I had a roommate, so I gave notice at the restaurant, too. Then I packed my belongings in boxes and shoved them in the closet of my room. I told my roommate that she could get another roomie, and I'd pick up my stuff later. I know it seems like I left her in a bad position, but I gave her the names of two girls who wanted to move in; but she will probably have her boyfriend move in. That was really more information than you needed or wanted." What he likely wanted to know was whether or not she was going to stay and if he could depend on her. "Bottom line is, I have nothing pressing I need to get back for."

He stared at her a moment. "I noticed in the meeting that you took notes in shorthand. Do you also type?"

She sat up straighter. "Seventy words per minute. No, that's probably not true. I'm rusty, so it's more likely between fifty-five and sixty. But if you have me do a lot of typing, I'll get back up to seventy in no time."

He pointed to his desk. "Use my computer and type up your notes from the meeting. I'm going to get you in the system so you can receive a paycheck." He picked up the forms she'd filled out earlier and left.

six

"Mr. Thurough."

Dillon detoured from his path across the lobby and walked to Henry who stood at the front doors to the hotel. "What can I do for you, Henry?"

"It's what I can do for you, sir."

"Henry, you really don't have to call me *sir*. *Dillon* will do."

"No, sir. I respect your position and authority. I won't disrespect you by calling you by your first name."

He had been trying for three years to get Henry to use his first name and always received the same answer. Maybe it was time he gave up trying. He'd learned in those three years that Henry could be quite stubborn about things he believed in. "What is it you want to do for me?"

"I heard that Miss Mikkelson is in need of a place to stay."

He took a slow breath. Yes, he still had the Aimee problem to deal with. "Where did you hear that?" News was traveling fast in the hotel today. And Henry always managed to know things first.

Henry smiled. "Oh, here and there."

"Mr. Howard just hired her this morning, and she will need lodging before nightfall."

Henry leaned closer as if the next bit of information was a secret. "I have just the place."

He smiled. "She can't stay with you, Henry."

Henry stood up straight. "Constance would have my head."

Of course she would. Constance was well liked by everyone

on the island. . .especially Henry. "Where do you have in mind?"

"With my Constance. She has extra space at her house, and she does get lonesome by herself. She would like the company."

Even if the company talks nonstop?

"Shall I ask Constance if she'd be open to it? I could ask her on my lunch break."

"Why don't you use the house phone and call her right now, and we can have this whole thing settled." And he could have his place back.

"No, sir. I haven't left my post for sixty years except for my regular breaks." Henry turned up his wrist to look at his watch. "I go to lunch in forty-two minutes. I'll talk to Constance then."

If they had reliable cell phone reception on the island, he would have one and let Henry use that. Lunchtime would be soon enough.

He knew Henry was practically a permanent fixture at the front of this hotel. But sixty years? "Henry, you must have started working here when you were a baby to have been here that long."

"I started when I was twelve. The regular doorman fell sick, and I was asked to fill in until he recovered."

"What happened when he came back?"

"He didn't pull through. No one said a word about replacing me." A smile pulled at his mouth. "I guess I'm still filling in."

Dillon laughed. "Let me know what Constance says."

"Yes, sir."

He turned away, then back. "Henry, may I ask you a personal question?"

"Of course, sir."

"When are you going to marry her?"

"When she says yes."

"Playing hard to get?"

"Harder than my first wife." A sly smile slid across Henry's face, and he leaned in a little closer. "But I'm going to wait her out."

Maybe Henry had met his match in the stubborn department.

Having Aimee stay at Constance Mayhew's would solve the problem of giving Aimee an advance. He wasn't sure he liked the idea of doing that, anyway, and it wasn't likely the hotel would advance her money; so that would leave him to give her a loan. She said she was staying, but would she really?

When he opened his office door, Aimee was twirling around in his desk chair. "Having fun?"

She stopped. "I didn't know what to do. I promised not to roam around the hotel, so I thought it best if I stayed in your office. The typing didn't take that long. I typed up your notes, as well."

"You didn't have to do that."

"I know, but there was nothing else to do. And it gave me a good idea of what you thought was important in the meeting. Then I thought I might organize your files and straighten up your desk. . . ."

His insides twisted. No, she didn't.

"But they are so neat and orderly I think they might be sanitized. I did water Gomer. And when I got tired of twiddling my thumbs, I started spinning in the chair."

"Gomer?"

"That's what I named your plant."

She named his plant? He was tempted to ask her how she knew it was a boy but decided against it. "May I have my chair back?"

She jumped up. "Oh, sure. What do you want me to do now?" She walked around the desk and sat in the chair opposite his.

Dillon sat after she did. "I'd like to print out your notes and review them. Then go over the festival."

"I printed a copy for each of us, both mine and yours." She pointed to a blank file on his desk. "There."

He opened the folder and read the first paragraph of her notes, then flipped through the stapled pages. "Did you write down the meeting word-for-word?"

She shrugged. "No one talked that fast. I got really good at shorthand in college. When it came time to study for a midterm or final, I had everything the professor said. I was in several study groups because I took such thorough notes. But none of that really matters here. Yes, I took the meeting down almost verbatim." She folded her hands and bit the corner of her bottom lip.

He had to smile. There was no shortage of information from her. He was getting to know her from her little stories that seemed to fall out of her mouth. "Let's just go over the highlights of the festival. The hotel hosts a concert in Marquette Park for the opening ceremonies, a Grand Hotel history lecture, a garden tour of the grounds, and the Lilac Festival Golf Tournament. You and I will be expected at each of these events. Mr. Howard would also like a supportive presence from the hotel at as many of the other events as possible. That means you and me. Because the golf tournament takes place on our golf course, you will be working with Steve, as well as myself, on that one."

❧

Once again, Aimee sat in Dillon's office alone with nothing to do. She really wanted to go looking around the hotel to see if anything sparked some new idea. Her search couldn't be over so soon. Something still had to be here. But she had promised Dillon that she wouldn't roam around, and it was a promise she intended to keep.

After Dillon had gone over the times of the festival events and what he needed her to do for each one, he had taken her to lunch in the staff lounge, bought her a club sandwich, chips, and a soda. Now it was the middle of the afternoon, and she still didn't have a place to sleep tonight. Maybe he was working on her advance right now? She would really like to know how much it was, so she'd know what she could afford.

Dillon backed into his office lugging one end of a table with Steve at the other end. "Set it down here. If we turn my desk perpendicular to where it is now, Aimee's workstation will fit up against it."

Her workstation? So he was going to keep her on as his assistant. "Can I help?"

"Could you move my chair out of the way? I'd have you move it out into the hall, but we kind of have that blocked."

She rolled his chair into the corner. "My own place to work?"

"I thought it would be easier for you to work if you had something to work on."

"Will it fit in here?" The table wasn't as big as his desk, but it would be her own space.

"There was no place else to put you, and since this is a temporary job, this will have to do for the time being."

And he could keep an eye on her. But she didn't sense that was his reason for putting a table in his office for her. She would work hard and prove to him that she was the right person for the job.

After Dillon and Steve had arranged the furniture, which, in the end, fit nicely into the small office, Dillon went to get her a laptop computer to use. Steve remained with her. "We have many nice places to eat on the island. Where would you like to go for dinner tonight?"

She rubbed her hands on the arms of the chair behind her desk. Her own work area and chair. "Are you asking me out?" She already knew the answer to that.

He sat on the corner of her desk and flashed the most charming smile. "I am."

That was a great smile. Dark hair, dark eyes, he was a package hard to resist. But she must.

"I'm sorry. I have plans." She had her workday to finish, find a place to stay, move in her belongings, and unpack. Then she needed to decide what to wear tomorrow and how to shuffle her three dresses so she didn't look like she was wearing the same things over and over—which is exactly what she would be doing. Dinner would be a rush at best.

"Tomorrow night then?"

"I need time to get myself settled before I think about going out."

"So, a rain check?"

How could she tell him no without causing waves between them? She had to work with this man, and it wouldn't be good for there to be tension between them because she rejected him. "Maybe."

His smile widened, and he rapped his knuckles on the top of the table before standing. "I'll take that as a yes."

He would. She smiled back.

He strutted out, and a moment later, Dillon entered their office. She liked the sound of that: *their office.* A part ownership in this little room gave her a sense of importance, even if it was only for a short time.

🙠

Dillon placed the leather computer case he was carrying on the edge of her table. "Was Steve here the whole time I was gone?" He wasn't gone that long, but now he wished he hadn't told Steve to feel free to pursue her.

She nodded. "He asked me out."

That could cause problems. "Aimee, Steve is not like you and me. I'm assuming that you are a Christian." She nodded again. "Steve isn't. Don't get me wrong; he's a nice guy. I've been witnessing to him. But if you go out with him, he may expect more than a simple good night."

Aimee cocked her head slightly to one side, and her features softened. "That is so sweet of you to care like that. I told him I had plans tonight, which I do. I need to find a place to stay and unpack, but we can talk about that in a minute. I told him no for tomorrow night, as well, and that I needed some time to settle in. He asked for a rain check. I said maybe, which he took for a yes. It puts me in a real dilemma. I don't want to go out with him, but I also have to work with him. So how do I tell him no without ruining our working relationship?"

Well, that was a relief; she didn't want to date Steve. She was right about the situation potentially getting sticky if not handled carefully. "I'll talk to Steve and tell him you're off-limits as long as you're working for me." He could play the heavy, and any problems Steve had with it would be between the two of them.

"Really?" Her beautiful blue eyes widened. "That would be so great of you if you would do that. I really didn't want things to be awkward and weird."

He suspected that any working relationship with Aimee would be a little. . .unusual. "I'll take care of it."

"You are the best boss." She smiled. "Can I ask another favor?"

It couldn't hurt to ask. He nodded.

"Could I possibly get that advance, so I can find a place to stay?"

"You haven't worked at the hotel even a full day. I'm afraid an advance is out of the question, but it won't be necessary."

"Dillon, you have been great about all this, but I can't stay at your place again and kick you out. I have to find a place of my own. Do you think this hotel or some other one would let me stay until I get paid with the promise to pay? Maybe if you wrote a letter of recommendation or something."

"That won't be necessary. Constance Mayhew has room at her house and has agreed to let you stay with her."

"You mean that nice lady with Henry I met at church yesterday morning?"

He nodded. "I'll take you over after work."

Her face broke into a genuine appreciative smile. "You are the best."

⁂

When the coach driver pulled up in front of a blue two-story house with white gingerbread moldings that looked like lace in the eaves, Aimee just stared up at it. People really lived in these cute houses? She had thought they were merely decorative, like in a Wild West ghost town.

Dillon opened the door to the coach and stepped down before holding his hand out for Aimee. She took it and stepped down onto the sidewalk. A white picket fence surrounded the yard, and an array of colorful flowers lined the walk and flower boxes at every window. Lilac bushes stood at attention on either side of the gate. They were heavy with blooms preparing to open within the next week or so.

Dillon opened the gate. "After you."

As she walked up toward the door, Dillon followed, wheeling her suitcases behind him.

Constance opened the door. She wore a muted teal dress with a white cardigan sweater. "Miss Aimee, it's so nice to have you grace my home." Henry stood at her side. A little white dog came out and sniffed Aimee's feet.

Dillon came in with her suitcases. "Where do you want these?"

"The upstairs bedroom. Henry, would you show him?" Henry and Dillon disappeared up the stairs.

Aimee knelt down and held out her hand to the dog. "What's his name?" The little white terrier backed away and barked.

"Samuel Clemens. He responds to Sammy. He's a little shy at first, but he'll warm up to you soon enough."

She stood back up. She would make friends with Sammy later. "Thank you so much for letting me stay here. You don't know how much it means to me."

"I have had seasonal employees here from time to time. I am particular about my boarders, but it's nice to have a young person around."

Aimee looked at the floor, then back at her hostess. "I know it's unpleasant to talk about, but Dillon didn't tell me how much rent will be. And did he tell you I haven't gotten paid yet, so I can't pay you anything until I get my first paycheck?"

Constance smiled. "Don't worry about it, dear. You pay whatever you feel is right."

"What if I don't pay what you are expecting? I don't want to take advantage of you. What have others paid in the past?"

"You are not others. You're a friend of Henry's. How about if I expect no money, just companionship, a little light cleaning, and you prepare a meal or two for us a week? How does that sound?"

"Too good to be true." This woman was holding out a charitable hand to her. Would it do any good to argue with her? *Probably not.* Aimee would do all the things Constance asked, as well as pay rent, even if she had to smuggle it into the woman's purse or leave it under the sugar canister at the end of her stay.

Henry and Dillon came back down the stairs. Dillon said, "Mrs. Mayhew, you have a very nice place here."

"It belonged to my first husband. He was an only child, so it passed on to me."

Henry winked at Constance. What was that about?

Henry gave Constance a peck on the cheek. "I'm going to ride back with Mr. Thurough. I'll see you tomorrow."

"I look forward to it," Constance said.

Aimee raised a questioning eyebrow to Dillon, but he just smiled and left with Henry.

"Isn't Henry coming back?"

"Back?"

"Doesn't he live here?"

"Oh no, dear."

"I thought the two of you were married. When I saw you together at church, I just thought you were a couple. A very cute couple."

"A couple, yes. Married, no."

"Now I'm really confused. You two appear to be in love."

"We are. Are you hungry?"

She stared at her hostess's retreating form, little Sammy at her heels. "Yes, I am hungry." She followed Constance into the kitchen.

Constance opened the refrigerator. "Ham sandwich?"

Constance and Henry's relationship was obviously off-limits. "I would love one. What can I do to help?"

Aimee buttered the bread and washed some lettuce, and after the sandwiches were made, the two of them sat at the table.

Constance said the blessing. Then, when she raised her

head, she said, "We have to get to know each other, dear."

Aimee wasn't sure if that meant they needed to get to know each other in general or if, after they knew each other better, Constance would be willing to talk about her and Henry's situation.

ɞ

Dillon took a deep breath before knocking on Steve's door. *Lord, please help me find the right words so as not to offend Steve.*

Steve, dressed in a golf shirt and khakis, opened the door. "You caught me just heading out. I have a hot date."

Dillon furrowed his eyebrows. "With whom?" Aimee had said she turned him down.

"Melissa. . .or Mandy or Melanie." He shrugged. "Something like that. I'll remember when I see her."

He already had a date when he asked Aimee out? Or had he made this date after she said no? Either way it didn't matter. "I have a favor to ask of you. I know I said you could show Aimee *attention*, but I'm going to rescind that offer."

Steve smiled. "So you're interested after all."

"No. I just think if you tried to date her, it could make the three of us working together awkward."

"Yeah, right. You're not blind, buddy. She is fine to look at."

He couldn't argue with that, but there was more to a woman—a person—than how they looked. "So you're not going to pursue a relationship with her?"

Steve held up his hands. "Hands off. I promise. She's all yours. Besides, there are plenty of other girls on this rock."

Fine. Let Steve think he was interested in Aimee. As long as the three of them could work peaceably together, that was all that mattered.

Okay. Maybe he was a little interested. But that still didn't mean he had the time.

seven

After living in Constance's house for the better part of a week, Aimee had fallen into the nice, slow-paced routine of the island folk, both here at the house and at the hotel. Only the tourists on vacation seemed to be in a hurry.

She had baked a chicken under Constance's supervision. Constance's idea of Aimee cooking a meal was to have her help out in the kitchen while Constance cooked. Aimee didn't mind. She enjoyed learning from someone who knew her way around a kitchen.

She set the table while Constance brought over the dishes of food. "Henry will pick us up in a carriage tomorrow morning for church."

Aimee sat. "How nice of him." Then she said the grace for their meal.

Sammy sat near Constance at the table, ready to receive the small offerings from the side of her chair. "Sammy likes you. As I do, as well."

Aimee forked a piece of chicken onto her plate. "Well, I like you and Sammy, too." Sammy had warmed up to her in about five minutes, and Constance treated her like a granddaughter.

"I'll tell you about Henry now." Constance dabbed at her mouth with her napkin.

So Constance wasn't opposed to sharing her relationship with Henry. She'd just needed time to get to know her first.

She had been dying to find out, and Dillon wouldn't tell her a thing.

"Henry asked me to marry him."

"Oh, Constance, I'm so happy for you." She gave Constance a hug. "When?"

Constance patted her arm. "Wednesday night while we were taking our stroll." She said it as a matter of course. "I turned him down again."

She sat up straighter. "Turned him down? Again?" Maybe Constance had lived so many years alone, she didn't know if she could share her home with someone else. Then again, she was sharing it with her just fine.

This house was almost as much Henry's as it was Constance's. He had his own chair and footstool, where he spent several nights a week sitting and reading the newspaper or a book while Constance puttered around the house. He had a little side table that Constance kept just the way he liked it. The only things missing were a wedding band and Henry staying the night. "Why would you say no to him?"

Constance took a sip of her iced tea. "Oh, at first it was for propriety's sake. He asked me to marry him on our very first date. It didn't matter that we'd known each other for years. Then it was a sort of a battle of wits."

How could love be a battle of wits? "And now?"

"I'm afraid if I say yes, he'll have a coronary. I don't want to lose him. I don't know what I'd do without him."

So that was her secret? She loved a man she refused to marry for fear of killing him? Was Constance just a chronic worrier? "I don't think your saying yes to his proposal will give him a heart attack."

Constance's eyes glistened. "He's not a spring chicken. And neither am I."

"You have to tell him how you feel."

"He knows how much I care for him."

She scooted her chair closer and took one of Constance's hands. "No. You have to tell him about your fears."

"Oh, I couldn't do that."

"Why not?"

Constance looked flustered and shook her head. "It's the way I was raised. Henry would probably just tell me it's silly to worry about his health."

"But it's not silly. When you care about people, you care about their health, too. You worry about him because you love him. That's not silly." She moved her chair back in place and took a bite of asparagus. "Do you want to marry Henry?"

"More than anything on earth."

"Then propose to him."

Constance jerked up straight. "I could never."

"Sure you could." She held up her fork. "You just say, 'Henry, will you marry me?'"

Constance settled herself back in the chair. "You make it sound so simple."

"It is. You already know what he is going to say. There is no risk involved."

"Unless he drops dead on me."

"He won't."

ae

Dillon sat next to Aimee in the church pew. He had gone with Henry in the carriage to pick up the women. Now, sitting next to her, he had the urge to hold her hand as Henry was doing with Constance. Instead, he curled his fingers around his Bible.

Aimee had done everything she said she would do. She was as good as any assistant he could ever ask for. She was a diligent worker and easy to be around. And he could tell she was trying hard not to talk too much while they worked, keeping her comments and words to matters relevant to the job. He appreciated that. And she hadn't gone off searching for nonexistent treasure every time he turned his back. In fact, he didn't think she had searched at all since being hired, except for that first morning when he took her to look. She'd made only a few comments about not knowing where else to look and asked if he had any ideas.

Aimee's hands lay one on top of the other in her lap, slender and smooth. She had a small amethyst ring on her right hand. Her birthstone? It was tilted a little off center. He could straighten it. His hand slid to the edge of his Bible; then he stopped and gripped his Bible tighter. He had to stop thinking about her. But how? She was sitting right next to him. *Lord, help me focus on You and the sermon and not on her.*

After the closing prayer, Dillon was relieved to stand and have the temptation of Aimee's hand out of his reach.

Their carriage driver had accurately anticipated the conclusion of the service and was just pulling up as they stepped out into the sunshine. Henry helped Constance into the carriage, then stepped back for Dillon to do the same for Aimee.

Dillon held his hand out for Aimee. She placed hers in his and climbed up. Warm and soft. He closed his eyes momentarily. He'd held her hand this morning after all, and now he was reluctant to let it go, but he did. He climbed in after Henry and sat in the only seat left. . .next to Aimee.

Aimee set her white purse on the seat next to her. "How about if the four of us catch lunch somewhere?"

"Woods has a nice brunch," Dillon offered.

Henry patted Constance's hand. "Constance and I are expected at Susan's, but you two kids go and have a good time." Susan was Henry's youngest child and still lived on the island with her family.

He wished he hadn't been so quick to suggest a place to go. He had anticipated the subject would arise of the four of them going out to eat, so he'd considered several places. Though Woods wasn't at the Grand Hotel, it was one of the hotel's establishments. He had thought Aimee might like it, but now he didn't want her to feel like this was a date or something. It would not be good to date someone who worked for him or with him. Wasn't that the reason he had given her not to go out with Steve? It would be rude to try to back out now. He would just have to keep it professional.

They drove to Susan's and dropped off Henry and Constance before continuing on to Woods. The interior lighting had a romantic mute to it even in the daylight. The large windows didn't offer much more light than the overhead fixtures because the building was shrouded in trees. He hoped Aimee didn't notice.

This was a business lunch and nothing more.

❧

On Sunday evening, the door chimes rang. Sammy gave his obligatory bark in case they hadn't heard.

"That will be him." Constance's gaze darted from the direction of the door to Aimee. "You answer it."

Henry had stayed at his daughter's house through the afternoon playing with his grandchildren. Constance had returned home shortly after lunch. Henry was due to return for the remainder of the evening. While he was gone, Aimee had given Constance a pep talk.

She stood up from her place on the couch, and Sammy trotted to the door. "Okay. Then I'll just leave you two alone."

Constance put a hand on her arm. "Please stay. If he has a coronary, I'll need you here."

"He won't." She gave her a nod and went to the door.

Sammy's tail wagged as though he knew who was there. Henry stood in a dapper, gray tweed jacket, white shirt, and his red bow tie. "Come in, Henry." Sammy stood on his hind legs and waved his front paws while hopping backward.

As Henry stepped inside, he leaned down and gave Sammy a treat. Sammy ran off with his treasure. Henry smiled at her. "Is Constance here?"

"She's waiting for you in the living room."

He followed her but stopped in the room's doorway. "Are you all right, Constance?"

Constance stood by the sofa. Her brow was pinched, and her mouth was puckered as though she had just eaten a lemon.

Aimee went to stand by Constance. "She has something to ask you." She turned to the woman who treated her like family. "Go ahead."

Constance took a deep breath. "Henry, you know that question you asked me last week and last month and for the past five years? I think you should ask it again."

Well, it wasn't exactly what she was supposed to ask, but the outcome would be the same.

Henry stared at Constance, then at Aimee, then back at Constance. He put both hands in his pants pockets, fishing for something, then turned and walked out the door without a word.

Aimee stared after him. What happened? How could he just walk out? He was supposed to say yes—or rather propose, since Constance didn't. She turned to her friend.

Constance's gaze seemed glued to the door, her eyes filled with moisture. "Well, at least he didn't have a coronary."

There was that, but this whole thing didn't make sense. "He was probably just stunned."

"He thinks I'm too forward. I've scared him off." She sank

back down onto the sofa.

Aimee couldn't believe that. Henry was so faithful to Constance. His love for her was so evident. Poor Constance. *Lord, if I've made a mess of things here, show me how to make it right.*

She sat down next to Constance. She didn't know what to do. "Can I get you a cup of tea?" That would give her something to do while she tried to think of a way to fix another mess she'd created with her big mouth.

Constance pulled out an embroidered handkerchief from the cuff of her dress sleeve and dabbed at her eyes. "I don't care."

She went to the kitchen and heated the water. Was the proposal/refusal all some sort of unspoken game between them? "A battle of wits," as Constance had said? Had she ruined it? The key here was Henry. She would go talk to him after she took care of Constance. She carried the silver tray with the china teapot and teacups on it and set it on the coffee table. After she had poured, she handed a cup to Constance. "I'm really sorry. I'm going to go talk to Henry and tell him it was all my idea—that you never would have asked if I hadn't pushed you."

Constance patted her knee. "It's all right. If it wasn't meant to be, it wasn't meant to be. I survived the death of my first husband; I can survive this." A tear rolled down her cheek.

But it was meant to be. She really, really believed that. "But you and Henry are so perfect for each other."

"I thought so, too." Constance sniffled, then squared her shoulders. "I'll talk to Henry tomorrow and ask him what his intentions are. I'll do it while he's at his post, so he can't run away."

They both turned at the door chimes. Sammy barked once and ran to the door. *Oh, please let that be Henry.*

Constance wiped her nose. "Who could that be?"

"I'll get it." She got up and opened the door.

Henry stood in the suit he'd worn that morning to church. . . with a fresh-cut bouquet of lilacs. "Miss Aimee, is Constance still in the living room?"

She stepped aside, wondering whose bushes he'd cut the lilacs from, and closed the door behind him. Sammy hopped backward on his hind legs. Henry didn't seem to notice him.

Henry handed the flowers to Constance. "These haven't quite opened up, but they are close. I know how much you like the lilacs. I first want to apologize for my rude departure earlier."

"Henry. . ."

"Please, Constance, I know I should let you go first, but if I don't say my piece, I'll bust right in two." He bent down on one knee and pulled a ring from his pocket. Sammy sat next to him looking up at him.

This was going to be good. Aimee took the flowers from Constance.

Henry scooped up Constance's hand, and Aimee held her breath. "Constance, will you do me the honor of being my wife?"

"Yes!" Aimee shouted.

Constance and Henry turned to her with raised brows.

"Oops. Sorry." She held up the bouquet. "I'll just go put these in some water." She tiptoed toward the kitchen but heard Constance say, "I would be honored." Aimee did a little happy dance over to the sink. *Thank You, Lord.*

❧

The next morning, Aimee swung Dillon's office door open. "I have the best news."

He looked up from the papers on his desk. "You found your family treasure?"

Ooh, that would be good. "No. But this is almost as good. You'll never guess what happened last night."

He took a deep breath. "Probably not. So tell me."

"No. Guess." This was too good just to blurt out.

He set his pen down. "You said I'd never guess, and technically I did make a guess that was wrong."

He was just going to be stubborn. She'd give him a hint. "It's about Henry and Constance."

"Henry asked Constance to marry him. . .again."

That was probably an obvious guess since he'd known Henry so long, but he didn't know the rest. She grinned. "And she said yes."

His eyes widened. "It's about time."

She pivoted into the chair next to his desk. He needed the whole story now. "It was so sweet. You see, I talked Constance into proposing to Henry. Well, he up and left, but returned with a bunch of lilacs he got from who-knows-whose yard and got down on one knee and gave her a ring. It was so romantic. Just like a fairy tale." She scooted to the edge of the chair. "And get this, he said that it was one of the few times he didn't have the ring in his pocket. That's why he left. He didn't want to propose without it."

"I'll have to give Henry my congratulations. I'm sure we'll be able to work something out here at the hotel for their reception. Have they set a date yet?"

"They have to call Henry's three children and see when they all can make it. Constance never had any children. So that means less people for us to juggle."

"I'll talk it over with Henry and see when he's going to shoot for." Dillon turned back to the papers on his desk.

"So, how would you propose to the woman you wanted to spend the rest of your life with?"

Dillon looked up sharply and stared at her a moment. "I don't know."

"How can you not know?"

"I've never had a need to think about it."

"Really? That's amazing. I know some girls who started planning their wedding in high school, some even in junior high school. I had friends who had a whole notebook full of their plans—their wedding dress, caterers, the church, even a general date—all they needed was their groom's name to be filled in the blank. So, now that you've had a little time to think about it, how would you propose? Would you buy a ring ahead of time or go together to buy one after you propose? Would you do it in a public place or maybe a romantic dinner for two?"

He took a deep breath. "I have no plans to marry, so there is no need to waste time thinking about it."

"You never want to get married?"

"It is not a matter of wanting or not wanting. It doesn't fit into my five-year plan, so there is no point thinking about it."

"You have your life planned out for the next five years?"

"I have a one-, five-, and ten-year plan, where I want to be and how I can get there."

She leaned back in the chair. "I don't even know what I'm going to do next month, let alone next year. Why plan so far in advance?"

"I like to know what to expect."

"That's not very exciting."

"If I don't have goals, how can I reach them?"

"And what if things don't turn out the way you planned? Won't you be disappointed?"

"I plan so I can succeed."

She opened her mouth to rebut him, then closed it.

"Have I finally rendered you speechless?"

She opened her mouth and closed it again.

He smiled.

She pointed a finger at him. "Don't flash those dimples at me."

He chuckled. "You have a problem with my dimples?"

"I have always loved dimples. I always wished I had some."

"Well, I'd give you mine if I could. I never did like them."

"You can't *not* like them. They're great. Dimples have such personality all their own." And so irresistible. She better get to work before she poked them.

eight

Aimee came in and plopped into her chair at her table-desk and stared across at Dillon until he looked up at her.

"May I help you?"

She wiggled her eyebrows at her cleverness. "You certainly may. Remember when I told you I'd come to you with any theories I had about my family's treasure?"

He took a deep breath, and she expected him to sigh audibly. Instead, he said, "Yes."

"I have a theory."

He stared at her, and she could almost hear the gears turning in his head. "Let's hear it."

"This hotel has several floors. The riddle said nothing about it being on the main floor." She counted one. . .two. . .three breaths before he spoke.

"And you want to search the end rooms on the other floors?" She nodded.

"Those are all premium rooms. They are likely booked. Maybe even for the season."

She flashed him her best smile. "Can we check?" He had to at least appreciate that she'd come to him first. She bit her bottom lip.

He turned to his monitor and clicked on the keyboard. "One is vacant until the guests arrive and check in, but that could be anytime. The others are occupied."

"Can we check the one?" She knew he still didn't believe in the treasure. But he would once they found it.

He rubbed his hand over his mouth and chin. "If we go now."

"Now works for me." She jumped up and held the door for him.

In the room, Dillon crawled around the floor of the closet as before. And as before, found nothing.

It took nearly a week for the other rooms to become free, one at a time. None of them yielded as much as a loose board. There had to be something she was missing in the riddle.

❧

"We set a date." Constance sat on the couch twisting her embroidered handkerchief. "All three of Henry's children can make it the second weekend of July."

Aimee sat down on the couch. "That's great. And so soon. Will you be able to make all the arrangements by then?"

"We're going to have a simple ceremony at the church with a reception at the hotel. Mr. Thurough is taking care of coordinating with the staff there." Constance laid her handkerchief out on her lap and smoothed it as much as the wrinkles would allow. She had worked a small tear into the side. "What if Henry's daughter tries to stop the wedding?"

"Which daughter?" Henry had two daughters and a son. His younger daughter still lived on the island with her own family, his son on the mainland somewhere with a family, and Henry's oldest child lived all over the world.

"Cookie." Constance twisted her handkerchief back up. "She hasn't liked me since she was seven, when I caught her digging up my flower beds and scolded her."

"You've known Henry that long?"

"And his first wife Barbara-Ann."

"She hasn't forgiven you for something that happened that many years ago?"

Constance smoothed the handkerchief on her lap again. "I haven't seen her since that day except at a distance in church. Once she left home, she never returned but a very few times, and I never saw her on those visits."

Aimee wanted to yank that handkerchief away from her but didn't think that would help alleviate Constance's fears. "I'm sure she has forgotten all about you scolding her and will love you. What about Henry's other two children?"

Sammy trotted over from his bed and sat looking up at his mistress as though he were concerned over her distress. "I wouldn't say they like me, but they do seem to tolerate me." Constance picked up her handkerchief and patted her lap. Sammy jumped up.

At least now, Constance could keep her hands busy with something else. "I'm sure they do more than tolerate you. I'm sure they will all love you, even Cookie."

"You don't understand. Cookie is a professional woman. She never married. I've never worked a day in my life. I went from my parents' home to Bertram's home. We have nothing in common."

"You have Henry in common."

"I just don't want this to cause strife for Henry."

"I'm sure you are worrying over nothing."

Constance's eyes rounded. "What if they all talk him into calling off the wedding?"

"That's not even remotely possible. I don't think anyone could talk Henry out of marrying you. Not even you. They'll love you, and the wedding will go on as planned." Constance had more worries than the island had lilacs bushes.

❧

Aimee had been watching Dillon for nearly two weeks now, and on the eve of the kickoff of the Lilac Festival, he needed to relax. Constance was right. He worked too hard. He was so driven and planned everything out to the smallest detail that nothing would dare to go wrong. But she had a special surprise for him tonight. She tapped lightly on his office door.

Still at his desk, Dillon looked up. "I thought you went home."

"I thought the same about you."

"I was just going over a few things to make sure everything is in order before tomorrow. But I think I've done all I can tonight."

"Good," she said. "I wanted to show you something."

He shut down his computer and rubbed a kink out of his neck. "What is it?"

"It's not something I can tell you about; you have to see it. Come on."

"I'm beat. Can it wait until tomorrow?"

"No, not really. It'll only take a few minutes. I promise."

"Very well." He stood and followed her into the lobby.

She stopped before she reached the front doors. "Okay. Close your eyes."

"What?"

"Close your eyes."

He took a deep breath. "I'm not closing my eyes."

"Come on. It will make the surprise better."

"Did I tell you that I don't like surprises?"

"I figured as much. That's why you plan so much. But surprises can be good."

"Predictability is good."

"Predictability is boring."

"I like boring."

"This surprise is good. You'll like it. Trust me. Now close your eyes, and I'll guide you."

"I don't suppose you'll let me out of this so I can just go home?"

"Nope. I'm not leaving until I show you. You're stuck with me."

He took a deep breath and closed his eyes.

She took his arm and led him out the front doors and down to the end of the porch. "Okay, you can open them now."

He looked down at her and held out his hands. "What's the surprise?"

She pointed toward Mackinac Bridge.

He turned.

Pinks and oranges offset the darkening sky behind the five-mile bridge. "Sunset."

His face tensed. He spun on his heels and strode away without a word.

She stared at his receding back. *What had just happened?* She knew he said he never sat on the porch to relax. She thought it was because he didn't have time, but maybe he worked so hard and long so he wouldn't have time for things like a sunset.

ॐ

By the time Dillon reached his apartment, his hands had almost stopped shaking. He went to the bathroom and took the towel there to wipe the sweat from his face and hands. He leaned his hands on the cold porcelain sink and stared at his pale reflection. A deep breath in. . .and exhale.

Surprises were never good.

nine

The next morning, Aimee headed toward the office she shared with Dillon. Would he be there? What would she say? What would he say?

She hadn't seen him since he stormed off the hotel porch the night before. She had wanted to go to his place and apologize or something but wasn't sure what had happened. She would apologize today. She took a deep breath and knocked lightly on the door.

"Come in."

She put on a smile and opened the door. "Good morning."

He looked up. "Good. You're here. I wanted to talk to you." He stood up from his chair.

She stood next to his desk. "First, I need to say something. I'm really, really sorry about last night. I know I did something wrong—I'm not exactly sure what and I don't want to pry—but I wanted you to know that I never meant to offend you. Please forgive me?"

The look in his eyes conveyed understanding. "I am the one who needs to apologize for my behavior. Running out on you like that was inexcusable. I'd like to explain. Would you like to sit down first?" He motioned toward her chair.

She backed up and sat.

He sat on the edge of his desk and faced her. "This is really hard for me."

"You don't have to explain anything to me."

"You deserve an explanation after my rude behavior last night."

She noticed his hands shaking but didn't want to mentio...

"When I was seven, my mom developed breast cancer. It spread rapidly through her body, and she died within the year."

She took in a quick breath. "I'm so sorry. My mom died, too, when I was seven. It's awful to lose your mom at such a young age." She felt an instant deep connection with him.

"Then you can understand the heartache. The one thing Mom wanted was to visit this hotel. We planned a trip, but she got too sick to travel. I told her that if she lived I would buy her the Grand Hotel. At seven, I didn't understand how impossible that was. She died, of course, but asked me to watch the sunset for her from the hotel."

A lump formed in her throat at his heartache. "So you wanted that to be special. Something you did alone with her memory. I can understand that. I never meant to intrude."

He shook his head. "I haven't done it."

She furrowed her brow. "Why not?"

He took a deep breath and blew it out slowly. "When I do it, I'll be saying good-bye to her. I'm not ready to do that. I'm waiting until I'm the general manager and am running this hotel. If I can't own it for her, I can at least be in charge of it."

That was so sad. He had kept his grieving for his mom fresh. He hadn't let go. No wonder he worked so hard. He was trying to sooth his guilt. "It's not your fault she died."

He nodded.

She saw moisture pool in his eyes just before it did in her own and blurred her vision. "Watching a sunset from the porch will not change your love for her."

"I know."

A tear slipped down her cheek. She wiped it away but doubted he noticed. She stood to give him a comforting hug.

He backed away. "I'm okay." He stumbled back into his chair and sat. "I'm fine."

Well, she wasn't. She could feel the tears boiling up at the grieving he was still doing because he wouldn't let go. "I need to—I'm going to—I'll be back." She hurried out of the office and to the ladies' room.

After a good cry, she returned. Dillon sat behind his desk talking on the phone. She sat at her table and pulled out the day's schedule to review.

Dillon hung up the phone and stood from his chair. "Show time. We need to meet with Ann at the tourism bureau to coordinate the details of this afternoon's concert in the park and make sure all the arrangements are still in place, no musicians out sick, etc."

She stared at him for a long moment. "What about all this stuff with your mom and the sunset?"

"I have work to do."

"So just like that, you put your mom in a box and forget about her?"

"I never forget about her, but if I let it paralyze me, I will never accomplish my goals. My mom is very much alive inside me every minute of every day." He held the door open for her.

So that was it? End of discussion? She took a deep breath and exited the office with him. Well, it was going to take her a few days to get over this. *Lord, please heal his hurting heart, even if he won't admit it's wounded.*

❧

The next day, when Aimee stepped into Dillon's office, she was wearing her long lacy pink dress. Had she forgotten? He had discussed it with her yesterday. "Did you forget what event we are attending today?"

She tilted her head slightly. "No. The 10K run."

"You're participating in a dress?"

Her smile slipped, and her mouth hung open. She stared at him in his T-shirt and running shorts. "I'm going to be in the race?"

"We both are."

She cocked her upper lip. "Do I actually have to run?"

"You can walk."

"I guess I can go change. I have a pair of green plaid capris and a lime green T-shirt with little bows on the sleeves. How long do I have?"

For her to go to Constance's and back? "Not long enough. Come with me."

He led her down to one of the hotel shops that sold the appropriate clothing. He talked to Della, the shop manager. "Aimee's my assistant and needs clothes for the race today. Can you outfit her down to her shoes and charge it to the hotel's Lilac Festival account?" He had felt a need to explain that she worked for him and what the clothes were for. The last thing he needed or wanted were rumors flying around about him buying clothes for Aimee and any other made-up rumors that would follow. He went back to his office to work while he waited

A half hour later, Aimee waltzed back into his office in appropriate race attire. She looked cute in the running shorts and T-shirt with the hotel logo on it. And if she didn't want to run, he would walk alongside her.

She put a shopping bag on her chair and swung a white tennis-shod foot up onto his desk. "See. Right down to my feet."

He handed her a camel-back pack.

"Oh. Is this one of those water things?"

He was surprised she knew what it was. "It is. It's easier than trying to drink from a water bottle or cup while you run. . .or walk."

Before the start of the race, they both did some stretches and warm-ups; then he stood next to Aimee in the middle of the pack of participants. "We can just walk, and we don't even have to finish the race. We can't place anyway. It's just for show."

"Did you finish the race last year?"

He didn't want to make her feel bad and wished he hadn't insisted that she come. He nodded.

"I can run for a while but not the whole time."

Steve came up beside them. "Hello, you two." He smiled and winked.

What was that about?

The signal sounded for the start of the race, and everyone started running. Steve took off and moved up in the pack. Steve was more competitive in the race than Dillon. Steve was out to win the race, even if he couldn't place. For Dillon, it was all about the job and making a good showing for the hotel.

Aimee fell into a smooth jog, and he matched her stride. He would let her set the pace.

After a half mile or so, she put her hand to her side and soon slowed to a walk. "Whew. I'm more out of shape than I thought."

"Do you want to stop?"

"It's better to keep moving."

"No. I mean quit the race. We don't have to finish."

"I'll be fine if I can just walk for a while. But you don't have to stay with me. You are obviously in shape for this. So go on. Catch up with Steve. I'll meet you at the finish line in a few hours."

"I don't mind walking." He enjoyed being with her.

They walked for about twenty minutes, then jogged for a

while, then walked again. The two-way radio in his pocket crackled, and he answered it. He was needed back at the hotel. "I have to go to the hotel. You can either press on or return with me."

"You mean I can continue this torture or go back to a comfy office chair and collapse? You drive a hard bargain, but I accept. Lead the way."

He smiled at her sense of humor. He was glad she was coming with him. "This way." He led her off the main route and headed for the hotel.

৯

Three days later, Steve peered in Dillon's office. He had a golf bag slung over his shoulder. "You ready, partner?"

"In a minute." Dillon began closing out his e-mail and shutting down the programs he had running. He enjoyed teaming up with Steve for a few rounds, even if it was only for show. It gave them a chance to deepen their friendship, so he could talk to Steve about eternity.

Aimee stood up from her chair across from him and spoke to Steve. "So you two are golf buddies, as well?"

"Well, the golf part is debatable. We hit little white balls in the grass." Steve chuckled.

"So do you think the two of you will win?"

"We aren't actually in the tournament—being employees of the hotel and all—but we play a few spectator holes to warm up the crowd and keep people entertained until the real show begins." Steve set his clubs down. "Hey. Since it is just for show anyway, why don't you take my place?"

She shook her head adamantly. "I don't play golf."

"Neither do I, really. What do you say? I think the two of you would make a great team." Steve's gaze passed from Aimee to Dillon and back.

Dillon stood. "She said no." He gave Steve a stern look. What was he up to?

Aimee waved her hands in front of her. "You really don't want an instrument in my hands that I'm supposed to hit another object with and send it propelling into the air. With people around? Not a good combination, unless you want to wipe out half the spectators."

"You can't be that bad," Steve said.

Why was Steve pushing this?

"Once playing tennis in high school gym class, I swung at the ball coming at me and, to my surprise, I actually got it over the net. . .three courts over. Hit Samantha Tillman in the head. Good thing it was only a tennis ball and not a golf ball. I'll pass. I really don't want to injure anyone." Aimee lowered her voice to a whisper. "Bad publicity for the hotel."

Once on the golf links, with Aimee in the crowd, Dillon elbowed Steve in the arm. "What was all that about trying to get Aimee to play? You don't like being my golf partner?"

"I thought the two of you would like to be together on this—spend some time together." Steve gave him a lopsided grin.

"Why? We spend plenty of time together."

Steve pulled a club out of his bag. "I'm just trying to help your little romance along."

That's right. Steve thought there was something between him and Aimee. "Why would you even care?"

He pressed a tee into the grass with a ball. "It's like this: You work too hard and make the rest of us look bad." He lined up his shot. "If your time and attention are divided between work and a girlfriend, it will give the rest of us a chance to catch up or at least close the Grand Canyon-sized gap a little." Steve swung and watched his ball fly down the fairway, then turned to him. "Distraction can be a good thing."

How did he tell Steve there was nothing more than a working relationship between him and Aimee without giving Steve license to pursue her? "Things aren't exactly progressing in the romance department. So, if you could tone it down and not push, that would be great." He put a tee into the ground and lined up his shot.

"Maybe I should have asked her to replace you in this little match so I could put in a good word for you."

Dillon stopped on his backswing and turned to Steve. "Don't you dare. Please stay out of this."

"I'm just trying to help."

"I don't need any help in this matter." He lined up his shot again and took it before Steve could comment further.

They both put their clubs into their bags and started wheeling them behind them before Steve spoke again. "You know what it is? You work too much."

"Is that your way of trying to get me to slack off on my job so you can get ahead?"

Steve shook his head. "Just trying to help you get a little balance in your life. Too much work scares girls off. You have no time to spend with them. Invite Aimee out to a nice dinner in town; not at the hotel—it will seem too much like a working dinner—someplace nice. Let her know she's special to you."

"I'll think about it." He had to keep things professional with Aimee. He could not step over that line with her, or he'd never go back. He would spiral down into that romance hole, and then where would his plans and dreams of running the Grand be? He would get so caught up in Aimee he would lose sight of everything he'd worked so hard to gain.

❧

Aimee stood beside their desks. Mardi Gras beads? Not a

spontaneous bone in his body? She found that hard to believe. Everyone had to be able to be impulsive sometimes.

Dillon looked up. "Are you ready to go to lunch?"

"Yes." If given the right motivation, she was sure he possessed some degree of spontaneity, some extemporaneous reaction.

He closed his folder and came to stand next to her. "I can't get around you, but if you move toward the door, we can both get out."

"Smile."

"Why?" A natural smile pulled at his mouth.

"Call it an experiment." Aimee reached over and poked her finger into one of his dimples.

He pulled her hand away from his face. "Why did you do that?" His hand was warm and strong around hers.

"I wanted to. I always wondered what it was like to do that. And. . ."

He studied her with squinted eyes. "And what?"

"I wanted to see if you were capable of doing something impromptu."

"I'm not. There are less errors and mistakes when things are well planned out."

She smiled. He was very capable of spontaneity.

"Why are you smiling?"

She marveled that he had no idea what he'd done. "Because you disproved your statement even before you made it."

"How so?"

"You grabbed my hand away from your face."

"That was a reflex."

She raised her hand, which he was still holding. "And this?"

His eyes widened slightly, and he released her hand. "Let's just get lunch."

She stepped out of his way.

Lunch was spent in relative silence, as was the rest of the afternoon. It wasn't really an uncomfortable silence, more like Dillon brooding over the spontaneity issue.

It was nearing the end of the workday, and she was ready to try her experiment again. Only this time, if she didn't succeed, she wanted to be able to go home for the day. There was more at stake this time. "I was thinking about what you said, that your grabbing my hand was just a reflex. Okay, I'll give you that one." She pushed out of her chair and came around to his. "But I still think everyone is capable of spontaneity at some point. I mean, stuff happens, and you just have to react. So let's test my theory. Stand up."

"Aimee. I still have work to do."

"Well, if you are spontaneous, this won't take long at all." She pulled on his arm. "I'm not going away."

He heaved a heavy sigh and stood. "This isn't going to work."

"Be positive. Say, *I can be spontaneous.*"

"I'm positive this isn't going to work." He gave her a smile, and his dimples pulled in.

So cute.

"I really need to get back to work."

She would ignore that for now. "Okay. It's really simple. All you have to do is do what I tell you when I tell you. It's that easy."

He sighed. He was exhibiting a great deal of patience and tolerance.

"Ready?"

"No. Can I get back to work now?" He tried to sit down, but she pulled his arm to keep him standing.

"Okay, this isn't something you would normally do, so you just have to do it without thinking. Because if it was something you would normally do, it wouldn't show that you can be spontaneous." She took a deep breath. "Kiss me."

His eyes widened.

"Don't think about it—just do it."

He just stared at her. He didn't utter a sound or even blink for that matter. And now he had thought too long. He'd thought, period. The moment had passed.

She swallowed hard. "You win." She left his office and headed for the ladies' room. Katie was just leaving as she entered. She tried to blink back the moisture so her colleague wouldn't notice.

She took a wad of tissue from the stall and dabbed at her eyes as she looked at her reflection in the mirror. "Well, Aimee, you gave it a shot." She had hoped by pushing him that she could break through the barrier with him. She had been sure all he needed was a little push to get him out of his self-imposed rut.

She liked Dillon more than she had liked a guy in a long time. More than she had liked Brent Walker, who sent her nephew to college. Dillon was the kind of guy she needed in her life to keep her feet firmly planted on the ground—at least sometimes. He knew what he wanted. He wasn't drifting. She was like a feather on the wind of God's breath. She didn't know where she would eventually land, but she knew God had a destination in mind. She had hoped it would be here.

Maybe it was somewhere else. She was tired of floating and just wanted to land someplace, even for a little while. Dillon had seemed like the bulwark in the wind.

≈

Dillon stumbled back into his desk chair. "You made a mess of that one, Thurough." *You could have kissed the only woman who ever made you consider altering your life plan. Instead, you just stared at her. You really can't do anything spontaneous.*

He dropped his head into his hands, raking his fingers through his hair.

Her spontaneity was that spark of life he had let go out when his mother died—a part of living he'd denied. Having her around was almost like being among the living, like glimpsing through the frosted window at the family sitting around the Thanksgiving table. He could see it, but he wasn't a part of the celebration. If he stood long enough, maybe he'd be invited inside.

He could do both, couldn't he? Pursue a relationship as well as his career?

ten

Dillon sat at his desk wearing a T-shirt and shorts.

Aimee stood in the doorway in a long, black dress. "Let's try this again."

"Try what?"

She sashayed to his desk. "Stand up."

He stood.

"Kiss me."

He cupped her face in his hands and obeyed.

He pulled back, and her eyes were still closed.

She opened them slowly. "Do that again."

He wrapped his arms around her and thoroughly kissed her, standing on the hotel porch at sunset.

Dillon sat up with a start, gasping for air. Where was he? He looked around his dark room. He swung his legs off the side of his bed and shoved his hands into his hair.

She was definitely getting under his skin.

❧

Dillon sat at his desk. . .in a suit. Aimee hadn't come in yet this morning. He kept picturing her in that black dress. She probably didn't even own a black dress. And she certainly wasn't going to ask him to kiss her again. Not after the way he acted. Or rather his lack of action.

Maybe he could goad her into daring him to do it again. He would make a plan of just how to get her to do that. He could engage her in a discussion on spontaneity and insist he had some and hope she asked him to kiss her again.

100

What was he thinking? *Professional.* He had to remain professional with her. Kissing her would not promote a good working relationship. Everything afterward would be awkward.

Either that or they would head down the relationship path. That might be okay—but it didn't fit into his plan. If he divided his time between work and a girlfriend, as Steve had suggested, he would slip in his job.

He looked up when Steve knocked on his open door.

"You alone?" Steve peered behind the door.

What was Steve up to? "Yes."

Steve walked to the desk. "I have some bad news for you." He lowered his voice to a conspiratorial whisper. "Pretty-Boy is after your girl."

Pretty-Boy was Steve's reference to the owners' nephew, Jovan, who had arrived last night in a flurry of people doing his bidding. And his reference to "your girl" must mean Aimee, since Steve thought they were an item.

Dillon hadn't completely ruled out that possibility.

However, Jovan liked to have arm candy wherever he went. If he didn't bring one with him, he usually picked one up here. Everyone knew Jovan was to be treated like royalty. Everyone but Aimee. He was to have whatever he wanted. But that didn't include people. "Aimee is adult enough to turn him down." He hoped she would.

"She did, but Pretty-Boy went to our boss's boss. He's talking to her now."

Aimee could speak her mind. Man, could she ever. She could talk herself out the situation. He wasn't concerned.

Well, not overly concerned.

❧

Dillon seemed a bit agitated when Aimee walked into the office. "You're late."

Maybe agitated didn't cover it. "Mr. Howard asked to speak to me."

The muscle in his jaw worked back and forth. "About what?"

What set him off? Maybe his mood was a reflection of her little experiment gone sour yesterday. She hitched her thumb toward the door. "Should I go out and come back in?"

He squinted in question. "What for?"

Wasn't he a barrel of fun today. "Never mind." She waved her hand in the air. "Apparently the hotel's owners' nephew is here and wants me to hang out with him for the day." And after yesterday and Dillon's current mood, she wasn't sure she wanted to be around Dillon today.

"You said no." His words were a bit terse.

Maybe it was best if she wasn't around him today. "I did at first. But Mr. Howard asked me to keep him company for the day as a hotel courtesy. He said it would be nothing more: show him around to the festival events, have dinner with him, and that was all."

"You don't have to do this, you know."

She was pretty sure of that but was afraid that Mr. Howard would find some excuse to get rid of her if she didn't, and that would leave Dillon shorthanded when he needed her most. She mainly didn't want to disappoint Dillon by leaving him in the lurch for the rest of the festival. "I know. Is it okay with you if I do this? You and I were planning on putting in an appearance at a few of the events. We'll just have Jovan with us." Was that a momentary glare from Dillon?

"I don't think Jovan had a threesome in mind."

"I don't either. But I can be cordial and polite." Even if he was being surly today. "So, if it is okay with you, I'm going to go meet him."

"Fine. Go. Just be back for the lecture at eleven."

Was that an order? She was planning on it anyway. "I will." She turned and left with the definite impression it wasn't really all right with him.

She walked into the main dining room, where Jovan Musser sat with a cup of coffee. His thinning brown hair hung in waves to his shoulders. He looked like a model or movie star. Could she just skip today? No Jovan. No Dillon. Just relax and shop all day.

He looked up at her and stood.

Too late. He'd seen her, so she walked over.

"Have a seat." She sat, then he followed suit. "I'm so glad you came."

"Jovan, about today."

"I prefer Jove." His voice, smooth like whipped butter, rich like Michigan maple syrup, poured over her. "And today is going to be great now that you have decided to join me."

She liked neither butter nor maple syrup. She preferred Michigan blueberry syrup. "I'm not sure I have. I don't want you to get the wrong idea. This isn't like a date or anything. It will be amicable-like. I'll simply be escorting you around for the day. Well, not like *escort*." She pulled her mouth into a grimace. She was making an idiot of herself. Maybe she should just leave.

He put his hand over hers. "I understand. Like friends. That's fine with me. I just don't like being alone on the island. I'm only here for today. I leave first thing in the morning." He gave her hand a squeeze, then removed his. "Shall we go?" He stood and held out his hand to her.

She took it and stood. "I need to be back here at the hotel by eleven o'clock."

His mouth cocked into a sly smile, and he winked. "A

beautiful lady asking me to bring her back to a hotel; I don't think I can resist that."

She put her hands on her hips and pursed her lips.

He held up his hands. "Just joking. Where do you want to go?"

She studied him for a moment and decided she believed him. "I don't know. I haven't seen much of the island. I've spent most of my time here at the hotel."

"Then let me give you a tour of this grand island oasis." He walked her up to the front desk. "Can you order me a carriage for the day?"

Katie, behind the desk, shifted her gaze from Jove to Aimee, then to the phone. "Do you want a driver, or will you be driving it yourself?"

"I'll drive."

She pressed numbers on the phone. "It should be out front in twenty minutes or so."

"We'll be in the salon. Have me paged when it arrives." Jove turned to her. "This way." He held out his hand and directed her.

Once the carriage arrived and they were aboard, Jove headed around the perimeter of the island.

"So what brought you to the Grand?"

She really didn't want to tell him about her nonexistent family treasure. He would likely offer to help her and even force the issue to help her. All so he could get something in return. He seemed the type. She would rather not find the treasure than have him feel like she owed him a favor. "I have heard about the Grand Hotel since I was a little girl. My great-great-grandfather was on the construction crew. I wanted to come to see all he had done." And what he'd left behind. "So why did you come?"

"Bored mostly."

"How can you be bored? Don't you like your job?"

"I don't have a job. Don't need one. I do whatever I want."

"That's why you're bored. You have no purpose, no direction."

Dillon had purpose and direction. And the drive to get where he wanted to go. So much so, people around him didn't seem to matter as much. He wasn't mean or rude; he just didn't let anyone inside his emotional bubble. He was probably afraid of getting hurt, afraid to lose them.

"So what makes Aimee Mikkelson so different?"

Jove's question pulled her away from thoughts of the one she wished she were with. "Different?"

"I don't want to sound arrogant, but women fall all over themselves to be with me. I'm never without female companionship if I don't want to be. I had to go to your boss's boss to get you to give me the time of day. I wanted to know why you weren't interested. Do you have a boyfriend? Fiancé? Husband?"

"None of the above." She wouldn't mind seeing what it would be like to be Dillon's girlfriend. But he'd made it clear yesterday that he wasn't interested in her that way. Having a break from him today would be good.

"So why are you resistant to me. What makes you tick?"

Tick? Was this an opportunity? *Lord?* "You really want to know what makes me *tick*?" She cocked her head sideways to look at him.

"I most certainly do."

"The Lord."

He raised his eyebrows. "As in the Lord God Almighty, lightening bolts and judgment over the world?"

"If you want to put it that way, yes. I think of His loving side. The part of Him who cares about every little detail of my life. A God so powerful He created the universe and everything in it, yet still cares if I'm upset over an insensitive word or action. Who loved me so much He sent His only Son to die for my wickedness, so I could live with Him in heaven one day."

"I heard those fairy tales, too."

"And you chose not to believe?"

He shrugged. "I grew out of them."

"You can't outgrow God."

He gave her one of those I'll-humor-her smiles. "I have no use for religion."

"I'm sure God would have a use for you, if you'd let Him."

He chuckled. "I like my life the way it is."

No, he didn't. "Even if you're bored with it?"

"I'm not bored right now." He cast a sideways glance at her. "You want to stop and get out? Walk around?"

She turned up her wrist to look at her watch. It was getting close to eleven. "Actually, can we pick up the pace and go faster?"

"What's the hurry?"

"I'm supposed to be back by eleven for the historical lecture."

"Boring."

She chuckled. "It doesn't matter. I'm supposed to be there."

"I could call the hotel and have you relinquished of all your duties for the day."

She already was, but she didn't want to tell him that. "I want to go to this. The hotel is important to me."

He smiled, then snapped the reins. The horse started trotting, and they pulled up in front of the hotel at one minute to eleven.

"Hold that carriage for me until we return," Jove ordered Kevin at the doors. It was Wednesday and Henry's day off. She was glad for that for some reason. She guessed she didn't want Henry to see her with Jove.

She rushed to the room where the lecture was to be held and slipped in just as the speaker was beginning his presentation. Aimee slid in next to Dillon in the last row that was nearly empty. "Sorry for cutting it so close."

Jove sat next to her. He reached across her and shook Dillon's hand. "It was my fault."

Dillon gave a quick nod of acknowledgment and focused back on the speaker.

After about five minutes, Jove leaned toward her ear. "Are you bored yet?"

"No," she whispered back.

After another minute, he asked again, "How about now?"

Dillon turned and gave her a stern look.

"No." She tried to shush Jove with a glance.

Jove gave her a puppy-dog look. He wasn't going to give up until they left. Besides, she would likely miss half the lecture anyway, with him either talking or pouting.

❧

Dillon watched Aimee leave. He wished he were the one leaving with her instead of someone else. Maybe if he hadn't scorned her when she asked to be kissed, she wouldn't be so eager to have fun with Jovan all day.

He wanted to kiss her. He had wanted to kiss her for a long time. But his plans. . .his goals. She was not a part of them. He touched the chair she'd been sitting in. He liked having her next to him. Maybe he needed to alter his plans, make new one-, five-, and ten-year plans. *Lord, show me what to do.*

He turned his attention back to the lecture as the speaker was talking about the renovation in 1897 when the west wing was extended.

That was it! They hadn't found the treasure in any of the end rooms because they weren't the end rooms in 1887 when the hotel was built. The west wing was added ten years later.

He started to stand. He wanted to tell her. He lowered himself back down. She was out with Pretty-Boy. Why hadn't he told her not to spend the day with him? And if she still wanted to go, he could have told her he didn't want her to go—that he didn't want her off with another man.

But he hadn't. He had his goals. . .his plans. Aimee wasn't part of his plans.

At least, not yet.

۰

Aimee sat in one of the white wicker rockers lining the porch. Jove's coat was tucked around her. Jove had pulled up another chair next to hers and sat down. They looked out across the hotel grounds and the water to the long expanse of bridge in front of the fading sunset. Though the colors were intense, she just couldn't seem to enjoy the view.

She wished Dillon were the one next to her. But this wasn't a place she'd ever be with Dillon, because Dillon's plans didn't afford him the time to come and sit. And then there was always the problem of him avoiding the porch at sunset. If his mom was able to look down from heaven and see him, she would probably be sad that he couldn't bring himself to do that one simple thing for her.

Aimee had drifted through the day with Jove—nothing planned, just deciding what to do next and doing it. She missed Dillon's schedules, knowing just where he'd be and when. Jove lived like her, from one moment to the next. Not knowing what was around the corner. Sometimes it was fun to see what surprise awaited her. But there were those few times. . . Not all surprises were good. She heard Dillon's frustrated words: *I don't like surprises. Surprises are never good.*

Sometimes they're good, Dillon.

She tried her best to turn the bad things around and see God's hand in them. Like yesterday when Dillon didn't kiss her. Then, today, giving her a way out from being around him in awkward silence as they both thought about the scene she had created. Clearly God didn't want her and Dillon to develop a relationship.

He had sat in the lecture like she didn't exist—like he'd rather not have her there. So, between Jove being annoying and Dillon being cold, she had left. Dillon's aloofness toward her was the hardest to bear.

The colors drained from the western sky, and the light faded. She should call it a night and send Jove on his way. But she wanted to enjoy the quiet of the night for a few more minutes.

Jove took her hand and caressed his thumb across her fingers. "I know what you said this morning, but. . .I could order a bottle of champagne, and we could drink it in my room."

She pulled her hand free. "I'll pass."

"Didn't you have a good time with me today?"

"Yes, I did." But that was beside the point.

"Then do you mind if I ask why you're turning me down now?"

She stood to go inside. "You can ask whatever you want. It doesn't mean I have to answer."

He stood, as well. "Is it something I did or said? I thought I was the perfect gentleman all day."

And he was proud of it. Like that could make her change all of her convictions. "I'm not the kind of girl who goes to a hotel room with a guy. And I don't drink."

"I sort of figured that, but I had to try. I just thought after a day together you might change your mind."

Not for him or any other guy. Not for his money or his good looks or his charm. "I think it's time for me to go. Thank you for a wonderful day."

"I'll get a carriage and take you home."

"That won't be necessary. I was supposed to check in with my boss before the end of the day." But she'd been avoiding Dillon, didn't want to feel his cold bristle.

"I think you missed that."

"He works late. If he's not still there, I'll leave him a note." She hoped he wasn't there and she could just leave a note.

Once inside the lobby, Jovan said, "You have made my stay on the island enjoyable for a change, even though you have resisted my charms."

She removed his coat and handed it to him. "I'm nothing special. You could have had fun with anyone."

"Don't sell yourself short." He lifted her hand and kissed the back of it. "An old-fashioned kiss for an old-fashioned girl."

Would it be rude to wipe the back of her hand on her skirt? Jove was nice, but she'd had quite enough of his charm for one day—possibly enough for a lifetime. He just wasn't the type of guy who interested her. Everything about him was right on the surface; there was no depth.

The next time—if there was a next time—she was asked to keep Jovan, or any other VIP, company for the day, she'd quit first before accepting. It just wasn't worth the hassle.

❧

Dillon watched from behind the front desk as Jovan kissed Aimee's hand and she smiled back at him. His insides twisted. What was this he was feeling? Protectiveness? Jealousy?

Aimee headed toward their office. He stayed behind the counter. She hadn't seen him there. After a minute, he headed for their office, as well. Aimee sat at his desk writing on a sticky note.

He stepped inside. "Oh, you're back. Did you have a nice day?"

"Actually I did. Jove was very pleasant."

Jove? That's not what he wanted to hear. He wanted to hear that she thought he was a leech and was glad he was leaving tomorrow. He was glad the man was leaving.

"We took a horse-and-buggy ride around the island, and—"

"I'm glad you had a nice time, but I have a couple more things to get done before tomorrow." He wasn't in the mood to hear about her grand day. To hear about Jove.

"I was just writing you a note to say I'm sorry to have missed you." She pulled off the little yellow sheet and threw it away. "Have you been working all day?"

"Of course. It's what I do." Actually he had been distracted since she left the lecture with Jovan. If he'd been able to concentrate for more than a five-minute span and string two coherent thoughts together, he could have been done early and home relaxing, planning the next steps to attain his professional goals. And possibly personal ones, as well. But all he could think about was Aimee with another man.

"What can I do to help?"

Leave me to my misery. "Nothing. I've got it covered."

Her shoulders slumped slightly. "Then I guess I'll go home."

Was she disappointed he wasn't going to work her into the ground? He stood. "Let me call you a taxi."

As they waited just inside the lobby, Aimee asked, "How was the lecture? I really wanted to hear it."

"Why didn't you stay then?" He couldn't resist the question.

"Jove didn't want to be there."

And what Jove *wants,* Jove *gets.*

He put Aimee into the taxi when it arrived and waited for it to leave.

The renovation! He forgot to tell her about the renovation. He would just have to tell her tomorrow. There was nothing either one of them could do about it tonight. The rooms were probably occupied. He took a deep breath. And would be until the end of the festival. It would be better not to tempt her with the information until they could get into those rooms.

He went back to his office and dug around in his files until he found a copied drawing of the original hotel floor plan. He took it out and studied it on all the floors. Once he figured out which rooms were the right ones, he wrote them down. He went back to his office and looked the rooms up on the computer, and as he suspected, they were all occupied. When the first one became available, he'd tell Aimee about his revelation.

eleven

The next day, Aimee sneaked in a side door of the hotel and wound her way through the service halls to get to their office. She didn't want to risk running into Jove and him pulling her into spending any more time with him. He had been nice, but she'd rather spend time with Dillon, even if he was in a prickly mood, than wondering when Jove was going to drop another hint involving the two of them alone.

She walked into the office and sat at her workstation, but Dillon wasn't there. Instead, a pink box with a red ribbon sat on her desk. Was this from Dillon? She took the small card attached and read it. *Sweet candy for a sweet lady. Until the next time. Jove*

Did there have to be a next time? Could she possibly be rendered invisible? She lifted the lid of the box. *Fudge.* That much sugar would make her blow up like a whale. And the variety of flavors all looked like they contained nuts. A whale with a bad rash. She'd pass on that one.

She dropped the card off the side of her desk to the trash on her way out and took the box of sweets to the staff lounge. She wrote "Enjoy" on a piece of paper and leaned it against the box. It would be history in under an hour. *Sorry, Jove. Even if I wasn't allergic, I don't want to accept gifts from you.*

When she walked back into the office, Dillon was at his desk with his head in his hands, rubbing his temples.

"Are you all right?"

"Raging headache." He looked up with squinted eyes. A pair of glasses lay on the desk in front of him. "I'll be fine."

She hated wearing her glasses. "Your eyes aren't lubricated enough to wear your contacts, are they?"

"It would feel better to poke a stick in my eye."

She grimaced. "I know the feeling." She walked around behind his chair and started kneading his shoulders.

"Oh. You don't have to do that, but it feels wonderful."

"Didn't you sleep well?" She worked at the knots in his shoulders.

"I was working late, then couldn't sleep."

"You were probably too wound up from working late to sleep."

"Probably." He tipped his head forward.

As she rubbed his neck, she could feel the tension loosening. He really needed to learn to relax.

They both turned at the knock on the open door.

"Dill—" Steve spun around and headed back out the door before he even got one foot inside.

"Steve," Dillon called after him.

"I'll come back in five," Steve's voice filtered in through the doorway.

Dillon stood. "I'll be right back." He walked out the door.

She threw up her hands. *And Steve wins out over having your shoulders rubbed by me.*

She slumped into her chair and rested her chin in her hands. "He said he'd come back."

♦

Dillon knocked on Steve's office door. "What did you need?"

Steve looked up with a lopsided grin. "Nothing worth running after me for. Go back. We'll talk later."

"Can we talk now?"

Steve spread his hands. "Sure. If you'd rather be with me than Aimee."

Not really, but he needed to talk. He closed Steve's door. He didn't want Aimee happening by and overhearing their conversation. He pulled the flat card from his coat pocket and handed it to Steve. "That was on my office floor when I came in."

Steve read Jove's *touching* little note to Aimee. "What did Aimee say about it?"

"She doesn't know I have it."

Steve handed it back. "Ask her."

"She'll think I was snooping in her things." He put it back into his pocket.

"Tell her the truth. You found it on the floor. Hand it back to her and see what she says."

"I already know what she'll say. She had a wonderful time yesterday with *him*."

Steve shook his head. "Why'd you let her go with him in the first place?"

"It wasn't my decision."

"You told her not to go, and she still went with him?"

If he could turn back the clock, he would insist she not go. "I didn't exactly tell her she couldn't go."

"Why not?"

"I wanted her to turn him down on her own."

"Boom. Backfired on you."

"She saw it as a hotel courtesy. She wasn't going with him as a date or anything."

"Well, I'm sure Pretty-Boy saw it as a date." Steve leaned forward on his desk. "You need to do some serious romancing. Dinner, flowers, your own box of sweets. It doesn't really matter. You just need to show her you're thinking about her."

"I don't have time for all that. I have work—"

"Chuck the work plan. If you're serious about her, show her you care."

He couldn't chuck his plan. He needed the plan to hold on to.

"What would she like? What would be uniquely special to her?" Steve asked.

Besides tearing apart the hotel to find a treasure long gone? "I don't know."

≈

On her way back to the office from running an in-house errand for Dillon, Aimee was waylaid by Steve. "I'm cashing in on that rain check. Dinner tonight at Claire's Café."

"Steve."

He held up his hands. "I know. It's not like a date or anything. I promise I'm not trying to put the moves on you. Go with me as a friend, as Dillon's friend. I need some advice on girls."

"You promise."

He made an X on his chest. "Promise."

She studied him a moment. "Dutch?" She didn't want any misunderstandings.

He hesitated, then said, "Agreed."

Aimee prayed several times during the day about whether or not she should keep her "date" with Steve. He'd promised not to try anything, and she would like to put a good foot forward for the Lord. The Lord had not given her any indication that she should cancel on Steve.

She didn't have a lot of options in her wardrobe. Besides her three dresses, she had her capris and a pair of jeans. She ruled out the dresses right away. She didn't want to look like she was dressing up for him, and he said the place was a café. After sunset, the air cooled quickly. She might get cold in her capris. So she had decided on her jeans with a tie-dyed T-shirt and her white cardigan. Now she sat across the table from Steve, who also wore jeans. They had ordered their food, and their beverages had arrived.

"Okay, Steve, what's your dilemma?" She took a sip of her soda.

"I'm trying to figure what women like. For instance, flowers or candy?"

"You asked me here to find out if some girl would like flowers or candy?"

"Not any specific girl. Just in general."

What was Steve fishing for? "It would depend on the girl. Some prefer flowers; others have a sweet tooth."

He leaned forward on the table. "Which do you prefer?"

"What's this all about?"

"I honestly want to know. Candy or flowers?" He held his hands out from him with his palms up, as if weighing the two options.

"If you send me either, I'll send them back to you."

"I promise this is not like that."

"Flowers."

"Why?"

"I'm not much into candy. My grandma is diabetic so there was never any around. She put the fear of sugar into me lest I end up diabetic like her."

"That's interesting. I always assumed all women liked both equally. But there could be a good reason to choose one over the other. You're not allergic to flowers or anything like that."

"Being on Mackinac Island in June during the Lilac Festival wouldn't be a good place to be then."

"Right. So what's your favorite flower? Roses?"

"Steve, what are you fishing for?"

"Answer my question, and I'll answer yours."

Would the trade in information be worth it? "Carnations. I love their smell, and they look lacy. Your turn."

He nodded. "Interesting. I'm trying to figure out what makes a girl choose a guy like Jovan Musser over. . .let's say, a guy like me or Dillon?"

She waited for their server to set down their food and leave before she answered. "To be honest, I don't know why a girl would. Jove is paper-thin. What you see is what you get. He was very nice and acted every bit the gentleman, but other than money and good looks, there's not much else there." She poured ketchup into the side of her basket of fish and chips.

"So you wouldn't go for the Casanova type?" He picked up his thick burger and took a bite.

"I like to know there is more to a guy than what is on the surface." She dipped a fry into the ketchup and ate it.

"Good."

Why did that seem to make him happy?

His dark eyes pinned her. "So, if you don't care about either looks or money, what is the number one thing you look for in a guy?"

Was this an opening? "I wouldn't seriously date a guy who didn't have a personal relationship with the Lord."

He furrowed his brow in confusion.

"A Christian." She broke one of her battered fish fillets in half. Steam rose from it, so she set it back into the basket to cool and grabbed another fry.

"Oh." His expression opened back up. "I've dated Christian girls before. Why is it so important to you to only date a Christian guy?"

"There is a level of closeness you can only get with another Christian. It's hard to explain. You really can't understand it until you experience it. It's the Jesus in me fellowshipping with the Jesus in someone else."

A smile stretched his mouth. "You're right. It doesn't make sense."

"As a Christian, everything in life has a deeper, richer meaning. There is so much more to life than what you see around you."

"I'd like to believe that. But what you see is what you get." He took another bite of his burger.

"That's where faith comes in. What you see is only the tip of the iceberg. Under the surface of the water is a much bigger chunk of ice. Even if you can't see it or don't even believe it is there, that doesn't change the facts. It's there. God is there. God is here."

He washed his burger down with a swig of soda. "So let's say, for argument's sake, I believed there was more to life than what I can see. What difference does it make?"

"All the difference in the world. It's not that there *is* more to this world; it's what the *more* is. It's God. There is an afterlife following this one, and everyone will go to one of two places— a place with God or one without God. Without God is not a pretty place."

"So you believe in the whole heaven-and-hell thing?"

"They are both real places. Where do you want to live for eternity?"

He stared at her hard. "Where do I *want* to live?"

"It's your choice. I'd love for you to be in heaven with me. . . and Dillon and all the others who love the Lord."

He shook his head. "How did you turn this whole dinner around to religion?"

"It wasn't me. It was God." Sometimes God could use her big mouth for good. When she let Him.

❧

On Friday, Aimee stared at her computer screen and studied the letter Dillon had asked her to compose. She glanced up over the laptop. Dillon was staring at her again. He'd been quiet all morning, which was nothing new, but today it was a different kind of quiet. "I'm almost done with this one."

"Do you own a black dress?"

Where had that question come from? Not out of the blue. Dillon didn't speak unless he'd carefully planned his words. "Yes, but I don't have it with me. Do I need one?"

He shook his head. "Never mind."

"It's my wearing the same three dresses all the time, isn't it?" She stood and looked down at her pink lace dress. "It's getting tiresome. These used to be my three favorites, but I don't know if I'll ever wear them again after this."

"I like them," he said softly toward his computer screen.

"They're nice, but I'm just sick of them." She held out the skirt of her pink lace dress. "Maybe when I go into town over lunch I can find something that's inexpensive."

"You're going into town?"

"I have an errand to run. I can go after work if you need me here."

He paused. "You can go. What about lunch?"

"I'll grab something while I'm out. And I promise not to get too wrapped up in shopping and lose track of time."

"You've put in extra hours all week. Don't rush back. Take your time."

Wahoo! Permission to shop!

⁂

Dillon sat at his desk eating a sandwich he'd ordered from the kitchen.

Steve came in. "You're eating at your desk." He looked around the office. "Alone?"

"Aimee went into town for lunch. She had some errands to run."

"Why didn't you go with her?"

He shrugged and took another bite of his turkey on wheat. How could he be of any use while she shopped for clothes? And then there was the point that she didn't invite him.

Steve shook his head. "Flowers. She likes flowers. Carnations, to be exact. Don't get her candy. She doesn't eat it."

He swallowed hard on his half-chewed bite. "What are you talking about?"

"Aimee. She likes carnations because they look lacy and smell nice." Steve wiggled his fingers in the air.

"How would you know that?"

Steve smiled. "I have my sources. I'm just trying to help you out. Now I don't know what color, but pink would probably be a safe bet."

Give Aimee flowers? That would send her a message he wasn't sure he was ready to send. He could see her liking carnations. They were frilly like her.

"Or think of something else that would be uniquely Aimee, something that she'd like."

Uniquely Aimee? How did you get any more unique than Aimee herself?

❧

Aimee went into the office after returning from lunch and set her shopping bags on her chair. "I found some great deals." She opened the first bag and pulled out a short-sleeved white eyelet blouse. "I can wear this over my red dress and tie it at the waist. It will give it a different look."

She opened the next bag and pulled out a short-waisted rosy pink jacket that had a shiny metallic look and slipped it on over her lacy pink dress. "And a new look for this one." Lastly she pulled out a green, yellow, and orange sundress jumper. "This will go perfect over my green T-shirt with little bows—"

"—on the sleeves."

He remembered. She had only mentioned it that once, before the 10K run.

"I saved the best for last." She reached into the smallest bag. "Look what I found." She could hardly contain her glee. She carefully unfolded the tissue paper and held up a tarnished silver locket on a black velvet ribbon.

He squinted at it. "What is it—besides a locket?"

"Nonie's treasure." Or at least it would be.

His eyes rounded, and he stood, gingerly taking it from her.

"Turn it over."

He did, and she knew what he was reading. *To my beloved Lacey. All my love, Mr. Wright.*

"Where did you find this?"

Confession time. "One of the shops in town."

He looked up at her sharply. "And you believe this to have belonged to your great-great-grandmother? It can't be a coincidence with those names. This is great! Now you can keep it and take it back to your grandma."

That was so sweet of him she wanted to cry. "Actually I found the antique locket in one of the shops and had it engraved. Now I just need to find pictures to put inside it. Not that Nonie will be able to see the pictures, but she'll know if something isn't there."

His gaze slowly rose to her face. "You created a treasure?"

"I figured that you were right and whatever Grandpa Wright left here is long gone. I think Nonie will be happy with something she can hold on to."

His eyes got a sad look, as though he was disappointed in her.

"I just want to fulfill her dream." It was no good. Nonie would know it wasn't the real treasure. How Nonie would know, she had no idea. Nonie just knew things. Now Aimee really wanted to cry.

He handed the locket back to her. "You may not need to give this to your grandma. I wasn't going to tell you until after the festival was over and the rooms were vacated, but after you left the lecture, the speaker talked about something I'd forgotten. The hotel renovations."

She stared at him. Was that supposed to make sense? "I don't understand. What do renovations have to do with Nonie?"

"This hotel—the hotel you see standing today—wasn't all built in 1887. The original structure, built when Adam Wright was here, is only a fraction of the structure today. The east wing wasn't even added until 1989. There have been a variety of shops added, and the Millennium wing opened just a few years ago."

"So?" None of those had anything to do with her.

"The west wing was added in 1897. Ten years after Adam Wright left the island. The end of the hall was much shorter in his day."

She widened her eyes, and a smile stretched her mouth. "We've been looking in the wrong rooms."

"Exactly."

"Can we go look now?"

He shook his head. "The rooms are occupied. That's why I was going to wait until after they cleared to tell you. I know it will be hard for you to wait."

"It doesn't matter. I've waited twenty-five years; I can wait a few more days." She threw her arms around him and gave him a quick hug. She released him before he could hug her back— or before she was disappointed that he didn't hug her back. She left the office and went out to the lobby. She stopped and looked around. Where was she going?

She was supposed to be working, so she did an about-face and slunk back into Dillon's office. "I got so excited I didn't know what I was doing."

His mouth pulled into a smile, and his dimples sank into his cheeks.

She still wanted to poke her finger in them. But she wouldn't try that again. She sighed mentally to herself. This was where she liked being. Sitting across from Dillon in his office, even if she couldn't poke his dimples. "What's on the schedule for today, boss?"

twelve

The next afternoon, Dillon said, "Tonight we'll go to the drive-in double feature at Mission Point." Each year, they played the two movies filmed on Mackinac Island back-to-back—a Lilac Festival tradition.

Aimee shook her head. "I still cannot picture a drive-in with no cars. Isn't that some sort of oxymoron?"

"I've never gone either, but I've heard it's a lot of fun." He hoped this would be something "uniquely Aimee" that she would enjoy. Since she didn't watch his videos, she hadn't seen either of the movies. "Dress warm. It cools off fast after sunset."

"I don't have anything warmer than a cardigan sweater and that lightweight pink jacket I bought the other day."

"I'll bring an extra coat for you. I'll pick you up around seven thirty."

"In what? I can't see a bunch of horses and buggies lined up in front of a modern-day movie screen."

He smiled. "You'll see."

At seven thirty on the nose, he pulled up in front of Constance's house on a tandem bicycle. Aimee was going to love this. He knocked on the door, and Constance let him in. Aimee skipped down the stairs a minute later wearing a pair of jeans and the white blouse she had purchased the other day. She carried a white sweater over her arm. His heart thumped a little harder at the sight of her.

At the bottom of the stairs, Aimee turned to Constance.

"Are you and Henry going to the *drive-in?*"

Constance shook her head. "We're too old for that."

"Speak for yourself," Henry said from his chair in the living room.

Constance waved a hand in Henry's direction. "Don't pay any attention to him."

Dillon caught Aimee smiling, and he tried not to let his own smile show. Henry and Constance were such a great couple and about as opposite as you could get. Henry was laid back, while Constance seemed to be wound tight. He glanced at Aimee again. She was his opposite. The planner and the free spirit. If Henry and Constance could make a go of it, maybe there was hope for him and Aimee.

Constance continued, "Do you have your key, dear? I'll be in bed long before you get home."

Aimee patted her front pants pocket. "Right here."

Then Dillon said, "Are you ready to go?"

She swung on her sweater. "I can't wait to see what you're driving."

He smiled. "Well, you'll have to wait a little longer. Close your eyes."

She closed them and put one hand over her eyes.

He thought he might have to argue with her at least a little, as she'd had to do with him. He took her free arm and led her out the door and down the walk to the bike. "Okay. You can open your eyes now."

Her mouth dropped open. "Oh, how fun!"

What a relief that she liked the idea of the tandem. "Do you want to drive or ride?"

"Ride." She hopped on the seat in the back.

He climbed on the front and drove them to the Mission Point Resort on the east point of the island. He parked the bike and retrieved two coats and a blanket. Then he paid admission, and they found a place on the grass with the few other early arrivers. He'd wanted to make sure they got a good spot. A huge screen stood at one end of the lawn. Several rows of folding chairs were set up farther back, and people were laying out blankets in front of them. He unfolded the blanket, and Aimee took two corners and helped him spread it out.

"Do you want popcorn and a soda?"

"Sure."

He headed for the vendor and bought two sodas and a long plastic bag of popcorn. He eyed the cotton candy. Would she like some? No. Steve had said she didn't eat candy—a tidbit of information Jovan didn't know. When Dillon returned, Aimee was sitting in the middle of the blanket. He sat next to her and handed her the soda and popcorn.

She opened the bag and grabbed a handful. "I was curious why you chose to sit on the grass instead of in the chairs?"

Would she rather sit in the chairs? "I figured it would be uncomfortable to sit in hard chairs for four hours. If you'd like, we can switch."

"No, this is fine. I wouldn't have thought about the chairs being uncomfortable and would have regretted not bringing a blanket to sit on. See, that's why you do so well as a planner. You think of all the options. I would have just come, wiggled around in a hard chair all night, then woken up sore the next morning."

At least his planning didn't drive her nuts. That was a good sign.

Halfway through the second movie, he noticed Aimee shiver. He grabbed the back of the blanket and brought it up over her shoulders. He was about to pull his arm away when she leaned into him and stayed there the rest of the movie.

Once back at Constance's, he parked the bike at the curb and walked Aimee up to the door. She spoke in a whisper probably because of the late hour. "Aren't you glad you finally saw those two movies clear through?"

He actually was. "They were good." He'd thought they would be boring, but though one was a little silly and both were romances, he'd enjoyed them. Or was it the company?

She fished her key out of her pocket and turned to look up at him. "Thanks for taking me."

He swallowed and nodded. Should he kiss her?

She stared up at him a moment longer, then turned to unlock the door. She stepped inside and gifted him with a smile before closing the door.

His heart drummed hard in his chest, and he raked both hands through his hair. He needed to figure out what he wanted and fast. Did he want to pursue a relationship with Aimee? Or was it best to leave well enough alone?

❧

The day after the festival ended, all but one of the rooms in which the treasure might be hidden became vacant.

"I'm so excited I'm shaking." Aimee held out her trembling hands. "This could really be it."

Dillon gave her hands a squeeze. He was excited, as well. Part of the hotel's untold history could be revealed. "This is what you came for." He unlocked the door and let her in first.

He pulled out his pocketknife and knelt down inside the closet. He ran his knife along the board seams and joints carefully as to not damage any of the wood. After a couple of minutes of failed attempts, he backed out. "Nothing." He handed her his knife. "You want to try?"

She shook her head. "I trust that your search was as thorough as possible. If you didn't find a loose board, then there isn't one in this closet." They searched the other rooms with the same result. There was one room left, but it was still occupied.

The following day, Dillon said, "They checked out this morning. I've blocked the room so it can't be rented until we have a chance to search it." He held his hand out to her. "Shall we go?"

"Right now?" she snapped. "I can't."

He knew her schedule better than she did. She had nothing critical pending. Neither one of them did. Now was a perfect time. "Why not?"

"Maybe later." She got up and marched out of the office.

Dillon stared after her. What was that all about? Why didn't she want to search the room? The room that likely held what she was looking for? Something was wrong.

❧

Aimee strode to the front desk. "Katie, Mr. Thurough blocked a room."

Katie typed on her computer keyboard. "Yes. I see it."

"Could you unblock it?"

"Sure." Katie tapped on her keys. "Done." She looked up. "Anything else?"

"Can you put the next available guest in that room?"

Katie shrugged. "Sure, if you want."

"Thanks, Katie."

Aimee turned and walked to the front doors.

Henry opened the door for her. "Miss Mikkelson."

"Good afternoon, Henry." She headed east on the porch and kept walking down Cadotte Avenue.

❧

Dillon sat at his desk. Should he go after her? He would give her fifteen minutes or so, then go looking for her. When the fifteen minutes were nearly past, he looked up when a knock sounded at his open door.

Henry stepped over the threshold. "Sir?"

"Henry?" Henry had never come to his office before that Dillon could think of.

"I'm on my afternoon break. The doors are covered."

He had to smile. Henry was so true-blue. "I never doubted you'd leave the entrance unattended. Have a seat."

"I would like to get off my feet." Henry sat in the extra chair next to his desk.

"What can I do for you?"

"I just wanted to let you know that Miss Mikkelson left the hotel a few minutes ago."

Well, he wouldn't go looking for her inside the building then. She probably needed some time to herself. "That's fine. Thank you for informing me."

"I just wanted to let you know she seemed upset."

She had been upset when she left his office, and he still couldn't figure out why. "What makes you think she was upset?" He wanted to hear Henry's observation.

"She didn't smile when she greeted me. She always smiles. I didn't know our little angel could be awake without a smile on her pretty face. Is something wrong?"

Of course something was wrong, but he didn't know what. "She didn't tell me anything. I'm sure she'll be fine." He would give her the time and space she needed. She hadn't taken her purse, so she'd be back.

When Aimee did not return by the end of the workday, he became concerned. He had hoped to explore that last room with her, so he could unblock it to be rented out. He pulled it up on the computer to find it occupied. He headed to the front desk. "Who rented out the room I blocked?"

Katie typed the room into the computer. "Oh. I did. Is something wrong?"

"I had that room blocked so it wouldn't be rented."

"Yes. Aimee told me to unblock it and rent it out the first chance I got. I assumed that order came from you."

He was more convinced than ever something was wrong, but he didn't know what it could be. He checked his watch: two minutes to five. Henry would still be at the front.

Henry was holding the door for a guest.

"Henry, your replacement is here. Can I speak to you for a moment?"

Henry stepped away from the doors.

"Did Aimee return to the hotel while you were on duty?"

"No, sir. But there are other ways into the building."

Too many. "Thanks."

He went to his office and called Constance. "Is Aimee there?"

"No. She hasn't come home from work yet. I was going to show her how to make tomato, onion, and cucumber salad."

Dillon then called the stable and ordered a saddled horse to be waiting for him. He grabbed a set of two-way radios and headed to his apartment to change clothes. Once at the stable, he mounted the horse and headed straight for Constance's house. He took the horse up the walk with him. He didn't want to leave it on the street to get spooked. "Now don't trample any of Mrs. Mayhew's flowers."

He held the end of the reins and stretched his arm to ring the bell. When Constance opened the door, he asked, "Has Aimee arrived home yet?"

"I already told you on the telephone she wasn't here." She eyed the horse in her yard but didn't say anything about it.

He pulled one of the radios from where it was clipped on his belt, turned it on, and handed it to her. "Would you tell her to contact me on this when she gets here?"

He left and decided to ride through town and see if she was anywhere around. He wove through the upper streets and the main street until he came to the park.

Aimee limped along the sidewalk with her white high-heeled shoes in hand.

He dismounted and came alongside her. "Why are you walking in nylons? Won't they get a run?"

"They probably already have holes. My feet hurt, and I have blisters." Her words were dull and lifeless.

His heart ached for her. "What's wrong? Why did you leave the hotel? Why don't you want to go into that room?"

"I suppose I owe you an explanation." She stopped and sat on the short park wall. "That room represents my last hope of finding what Adam Wright left for Nonie. I'm not ready for it all to be over."

"What if everything you hoped for is there?"

"Then the hotel will have a 120-year-old treasure."

He understood. She'd resigned herself; she lost either way. By not finding the treasure, it still belonged to her grandma. Once found, it was lost to her. "I'm sure when we tell the Mussers your story, they will let you borrow it to show your grandma. They may even give it to you."

"What if nothing is there at all?"

"I don't know. But you can't go back to your grandma until you know. You can't give up."

"And I can't keep avoiding calling her. She probably thinks I forgot about her."

"I doubt that."

She stood up and started limping. "I should head home. Constance will be wondering where I am. It's nice to have someone worry about me."

He worried about her, too. "Your feet are injured. Why don't you ride?"

She stopped and held out the skirt of her red dress with white polka dots. "Because I'm in a dress."

"You can sit sideways on the saddle. And I'll walk the horse." He took her shoes and lifted her up. "Turn sort of forward and hold on to the saddle horn." She did, and he walked the horse to Constance's.

As he was guiding the horse up the front walk, Constance threw open the front door. "There she is." Henry stood at her side. "Oh my goodness, what happened to you?" Sammy trotted out and barked once at the horse, then raced back inside. Fortunately the horse didn't pay any attention to Sammy's abrupt remark.

Henry took the reins.

Aimee smiled down at Constance. "I went walking in the wrong kind of shoes. Blisters."

It was good to see her smile back. Dillon held out his arms. "Slide down. I'll catch you."

She put her hands on his shoulders and slid slowly.

He cradled her in his arms and took her inside, setting her on the couch.

Sammy jumped on the couch and stared at her. She scratched him behind the ear. "I could have walked."

But he wanted to carry her. Dillon turned to Constance. "Do you have anything for blisters?"

"Of course." She left and returned.

He petted the dog's silky white fur. "You're in good hands now. I'll head back to the hotel."

Constance turned sharply to him. "No, you won't, young man. You're staying for supper."

"I have to get the horse back."

Constance waved a hand in the air. "You can call someone from the stable to come and get her, can't you?"

Well, yes, he could.

"The telephone's in the kitchen. I'm sure you know the number." Constance turned to Aimee. "And you go up and change out of these clothes, and we'll dress those blisters properly."

Would it do any good to argue with her? Besides, he wouldn't mind spending a little more time with Aimee. He phoned the stable, then waited out in the yard with Henry and the horse until one of the stable employees came.

After supper, Aimee walked Dillon out to the sidewalk. "Thanks for coming to look for me."

"Henry was really worried about you."

"Henry?"

"Okay, I was concerned, too. I didn't know what had upset you, and then you didn't return."

"I'm sorry I caused all this fuss."

"It's all right." Would she mind if he kissed her right now? He wanted to.

The radio on his belt crackled. "Hello?"

He unclipped it. "Yes." But his word went nowhere.

Constance had the button still pressed. "I don't think this thing works. He said she could just call him on this."

He chuckled. "I'll be right back."

Then came Henry's voice. "You have to release the button so he can talk."

He opened the door. "I'm right here."

Constance handed him the radio. "I didn't know if you had actually left. Henry was going to walk back with you."

"I was just about to leave. I'd love the company." It was

best this way. He shouldn't be entertaining the idea of kissing Aimee anyway.

≈

Aimee stood with Constance and watched Dillon walk down the street with Henry. For one brief moment, she had thought he might kiss her. But then the radio blared. She didn't blame Constance. If Dillon had wanted to kiss her, he could have, but he chose not to.

When he rode up earlier, like a white knight on his fearless steed, it soothed her fear over possibly not finding the treasure. She had waited until he'd carried her all the way into the house before she told him she could have walked. She liked being in his arms. And that irritated her now. He obviously didn't feel the same about her. *Henry was worried.*

Constance touched Aimee's arm and brought her out of her thoughts. "They're gone. Let's go inside to talk. It's getting chilly out here." Once inside, she said, "Have a seat, and I'll make us some tea." Sammy jumped up onto the couch and curled up next to her.

In a few minutes, Constance brought in the tea tray, poured them each a cup, and then sat next to Aimee on the couch. "It's none of my business, but if you want to talk about it, I'm here."

She told Constance about the final room becoming vacant and not wanting to go inside it. "I just panicked and left. What if there is nothing there?"

"What if there is?"

"I just don't believe anymore that there is anything left to find. And if I look and am right, Nonie has nothing—not even the dream or the hope of the dream."

"We serve a mighty God. He can do the impossible and lavish you with treasure greater than you ever imagined."

Constance took a sip of tea. "Look at Henry and me. I never thought I would have this kind of love again here on earth, but the Lord has blessed me beyond my dreams. And if Cookie doesn't like me, I don't care anymore."

Aimee prayed that night that she could accept whatever she found—or didn't find—in that room when it opened up and that she would have the courage to find out. "You are more sufficient than any earthly treasure. Help me accept it, and help Nonie not to be too disappointed, either, if there is nothing there."

thirteen

The following Monday, the room was empty—as was Aimee's dream of finding something. "It's over then. There is nothing left here that my great-great-grandfather left." She stared into the closet.

"I'm so sorry. I really wanted it to be here for you."

She took a deep breath. "I decided that this was the end of the hunt and whatever was found, I would tell Nonie. I'm going to give her the locket and tell her I had it engraved in memory of Adam and Lacey."

"You're not going to leave now, are you?"

"I was only hired to work through the Lilac Festival. It's been over for a week now."

"But there are other events: the Arts weekend, all of the Grand Hotel birthday celebrations, Fourth of July, Labor Day, the *Somewhere in Time* weekend. There are events happening all season until the end of October."

"You want me to stay?"

"I need you. You have been a big help."

Her hopes dashed. It was only about work. Why should she think he would think of anything else? Nothing mattered to Dillon except work. "Would I still be working as your assistant?"

"Of course. I've come to depend on you."

Could she get him to depend on her for more than just work? "Can I think about it?"

"Only if your answer is yes." He smiled, and his dimples puckered in.

She wanted to stay. But what then? Would it be better to leave now and search for a new job? Or keep the well-paying job she had until the end of October, then go back to the real world for a real job? "I'll think about it. . .but no promises as to my answer yet."

&

When Aimee walked into the office first thing Wednesday morning, Henry was sitting in the spare office chair, and Dillon sat behind his desk. Both men rose. Henry wore his gray tweed jacket and red bow tie.

"What's this little powwow about?" She thumbed toward the door. "Should I come back later?"

Dillon shook his head. "Henry came to see you."

It was probably something to do with the wedding. "What can I do for you, Henry?"

Henry took her hand in his. "Miss Aimee, as always, it is such a joy to see you. Constance was telling me the story of your ancestors and how something was left for you. I hope you don't mind her confiding in me?"

"Not at all."

"She said you didn't find what you were looking for yet."

"Whatever Adam Wright left here is long gone." She had accepted it, and she'd have to convince Nonie to accept it, as well. "I bought a locket I'm going to give my grandma and tell her I had it engraved in memory of Adam and Lacey since I couldn't find the real treasure left for her."

He gave her a gentle smile. "Come with me. I have something to show you."

She followed him to a small cottage in the woods behind the hotel. Dillon came, as well.

Henry opened the door and let them inside. "When I took over this cottage in '52, it was in bad shape. I completely rebuilt the inside and added onto the back in '63, when our second child arrived. We just plum needed more space."

The walls were a robin-egg blue, and worn rugs covered polished oak floors. Antique furniture adorned the main area and the dining room. "You've done a nice job." Henry obviously wanted to show off his work. And he should be proud; it was beautiful.

"The hotel has gone through many changes over the years."

"So I've heard."

"They discarded some fine materials. Every one of these floorboards once lined the inside of the hotel. The furniture once adorned some room. And even the rugs, linens, and curtains were once a part of the rich tradition of the Grand."

"Wow. None of this looks as though it was someone else's castoffs." These floorboards came from inside the hotel? Beneath one of them, someone had found Nonie's inheritance. It really was gone. "You did some fabulous work here."

"Thank you." He walked to the front window. "Come. This is what I brought you to see."

She looked out the window but only saw the back of the hotel. What was so special about the view?

He pulled back the curtain beyond the windowsill. "This was Annie's favorite part of the house. Even when she was sick with child, she'd polish this board."

She looked the length of the board and sucked in a breath. Carved in the wood toward the end: *Adam + Lacey Forever*. The words blurred. She blinked several times before she could see them again. She gently ran her fingers over the carving. The treasure had literally been *in the wood*. "Can I take a picture of this? I know Nonie won't be able to see or feel it in the picture, but I can tell her about it."

He removed his coat to reveal red suspenders. "I'll do you

one better." Henry handed a crowbar to Dillon, and he took up a large screwdriver and hammer. "If you can get that end, Mr. Thurough?" Henry wedged the screwdriver under the windowsill, and Dillon did the same at the other end.

"What are you doing?" She grabbed the hammer Henry was about to hit the end of the screwdriver with.

Henry turned his kind gaze on her. "I'm giving you your treasure."

"But it is part of your house. Your home."

"Annie and I always knew it was never ours, that we were somehow borrowing it. Annie would want you to have it."

She released her hold on the hammer and let the two men pry the board off the frame. Tears flooded her eyes and trickled down her cheek.

Once the board was loose, Henry turned and saw her tears. "Gracious. You're leaking." He pulled a neatly pressed and folded handkerchief from his back pocket and handed it to her.

She waved it in the air. "I'll get it all wet."

"That's what it's for, child."

She dried her face, and Henry gave her the board. "Your ancestor left this for you."

"Thank you so much." She hugged it to herself, then set it aside and hugged Henry. And since she was in the mood, she hugged Dillon, too. His arms came around her briefly just before she released him.

❧

The next morning, she stood on the pier with her luggage and her precious treasure. Dillon had wrapped it and put it in a Grand Hotel gift bag.

"Are you coming back?"

She nodded. "I can't miss Constance and Henry's wedding next week."

"Good. We can talk about work after that?"

"I'm still thinking about it." She had thanked God for answering her prayer to have a way inside the hotel long enough to find Nonie's inheritance, and though He had by giving her the job, was she supposed to stay, now that her prayer was answered? Or was she to float to the next thing? Whatever that would be.

"I really do need you."

"We'll talk." She didn't want to make any decisions right now. A little distance and a little prayer and she'd have a better idea of what the Lord wanted for her.

He gave her a quick kiss before she boarded. She wanted to cling to him and never let him go. Was that a good-bye kiss or a please-come-back kiss?

She stood on the back of the ferry and watched the Grand Hotel shrink in the distance. She had come and found what she was looking for. So why did it hurt to leave?

❧

Aimee walked up to the nurses' station in the hospital wing at the EagleView Assisted Living and Retirement Center. The smell of disinfectant, bicarbonate of soda, and rubbing alcohol pricked her nose.

Betty looked up from a chart and smiled. "Aimee. It's good to see you again. Bad news." But Betty's smile didn't fade. "She's not here anymore. We moved her back to her regular room."

"She's doing that well?"

"She said she had to start getting around again so she could go to that island and find you. She was sure they did something to you."

She held up the gift bag. "I have a surprise for her."

Betty's eyes widened. "You found it?"

She nodded. "I hope she's not disappointed."

"I think she'll just be glad you're back."

Betty escorted her to the other end of the center where residents stayed who needed less care. Betty opened Nonie's door.

Nonie sat in a wheelchair facing the window. She turned her ear toward the door. "Who's there?"

"It's Betty."

She turned her face back toward the window. "I'm not taking any more of your pills. I'm fine and am going to fly this coop as soon as my great-grandson gets here." Her raspy voice sounded every bit her ninety-three years. Nonie was wearing out.

"I brought you a visitor."

Nonie turned back toward the door. "Is that you, Justin? No. He doesn't wear that perfume." She raised her arms up for a hug. "Muffin!"

Aimee set her bag by the bed and embraced Nonie. Then Nonie tapped her shoulder. "Shame on you for not calling. You had me worried."

"I'm fine. I'm sorry for worrying you." She had avoided calling because she didn't want to disappoint Nonie with her lack of progress. She had kept the calls she did make short and called late when Nonie was likely in bed, but she knew Nonie would get the message that she had at least tried.

"I heard a bag crinkle. Did you bring me some of the famous Mackinac Island fudge?"

"I'm sorry. I forgot." Forgot on purpose. Nonie knew better than to even ask.

"No matter. I'm just glad to have you back."

"But I did bring you something." She pulled the wrapped board out of the bag and laid it across Nonie's lap. "I found it, Nonie."

Nonie sucked in a breath. "I thought it was no longer there, and that's why you stopped calling." Nonie tore off the paper and ran her hands over the smooth surface. "It feels like a board. What is it?"

"Down here." Aimee moved Nonie's fingers to the end with the carving.

Nonie outlined each letter with her fingers.

Aimee's eyes blurred as she imagined each word coming together for the sightless woman.

A tear rolled down Nonie's cheek. "He loved her very much."

All she could do was nod, even though she knew Nonie couldn't see it. She pulled two tissues out of the box by Nonie's bed and handed one to Nonie and dabbed at her own tears with the other.

"So you found it. I thought it was probably lost forever. In well over a hundred years, a lot of things could have happened to this."

A lot of things had.

Nonie turned her face up toward her. "Was it still where Granddad left it?"

"The hotel has grown since the original structure Adam Wright helped build. In one of the renovations, this board was removed and originally left in a scrap pile that was stored until needed in any future remodeling or repairs. Henry, the doorman at the hotel—he's been there for sixty years. Can you believe that? Anyway, Henry lived in this little cottage on the back of the hotel grounds and used those leftovers to fix up his place. He had this in his front windowsill where his first wife lovingly polished it. It's just all so romantic. I wish I could have met all these people who have touched the history of the Grand Hotel."

"Well, in a way you have by finding this board and becoming friends with Henry. You have felt the hotel's heartbeat, its history."

"Nonie, I was thinking as I was traveling away from Mackinac Island. I want to write Adam and Lacey's story."

"Like a book?"

"Oh, nothing that would be published or anything. But this is our family legacy. I want to preserve it for our future generations."

Nonie pointed toward her dresser. "In my bottom drawer, there are some letters and Lacey's journal. Take them. Tell their story."

She hugged the old woman around the shoulder. "Thank you."

Nonie patted her hand. "Now tell me about your man."

She guffawed. "I don't have a man."

"Your boss. When you called to say you had a job and would need to stay on the island for a while, I heard it in your voice. He's special."

Dillon was definitely special. And he'd given her a hasty parting kiss. "He's a faithful Christian and has the cutest dimples."

"You always did have a penchant for dimples. Remember the time you drew black dots on your cheeks with a permanent marker because you wanted dimples."

"Mom practically scrubbed my cheeks raw, and they still didn't come off."

"She was so furious with you. Easter family picture and you with black on your face."

"I love that picture. My 'dimples' were just light enough to look like they might be real." She touched her cheek where one of them had been all those years ago. She wished she could poke Dillon's dimples one last time just to see the stunned look on his face.

৯৹

Dillon roamed the hotel, floor by floor. He came to rest at his desk and stared across at the empty chair. This place just wasn't the same without Aimee. Quiet and stagnant. Is this really what his life had been like before she arrived?

He missed the lilt of her voice as she spun off into some trite bit of information or a barely related story. But none of it was trite. It was who she was. It was hard to believe he'd only known her for a little over a month. He knew more about her than he knew about people he'd worked with for years. More than he knew about Steve, with whom he'd worked for two years.

And he'd told her more about himself than he'd told anyone else.

He should have told her how he felt about her. What if she didn't come back?

"I hope she gets back soon." Steve stood in his doorway. "I don't know how much more of your moping I can take."

"I'm not moping."

"You are, too. You're like a lost little puppy dog. If you don't tell her how you feel when she gets back, I will." Steve slapped the door frame with his palm and left.

Dillon went to his apartment and microwaved a chicken and broccoli something-or-other he had in his refrigerator. Though he knew the spices and seasonings Chef Tony prepared it with were robust and flavorful, he just couldn't enjoy the meal.

He glanced at his watch. The sun would be setting in five minutes. He set his plate on the counter and picked up the silver-framed photo. "It's time, Mom."

He took the picture with him and strode through the hotel but stopped several paces before he reached the front doors.

He could see the orange and pink hues filtering through the lobby windows, setting the furnishings aglow. He took a deep breath and did an about-face. Something wasn't right.

After going to bed, he couldn't sleep. He rolled over in bed. Sleep was elusive tonight. He felt like a fish flopping about.

Around one, he heard a knock on his door. Who could that be? He rose to answer it; he wasn't sleeping anyway.

Steve stood outside his door. "Did I wake you?"

Normally he'd say yes. He rubbed his hands over his face. "I couldn't sleep. You want to come in?"

Steve came in and sat on his couch. "Can you tell me what's under the iceberg we can see?"

Huh?

fourteen

Aimee stepped off the ferry. It felt good to be back. She filled her lungs with the Mackinac air and regretted it. She had forgotten about the pungent horse aroma that had become dominant after the lilacs faded.

She approached a young woman holding a piece of paper with her name on it. "I'm Aimee Mikkelson."

The girl smiled. "The hotel has sent a private carriage. I'll grab your luggage."

Wow. That was really nice of them. Was Dillon behind it? She pointed out her two suitcases, and the girl carried them.

As they approached a carriage, Jovan stepped down out of it. "Sunshine."

Her shoulders slumped. If anyone was going to meet her, why did it have to be Jovan?

"Welcome back." He stopped in front of her.

She tried not to sigh audibly. "Hello."

The girl secured her suitcases to the back of the carriage.

How rude would it be to remove her suitcases from his carriage and put them on the Grand Hotel coach? He had gone to the trouble of getting a carriage and had waited for who knows how long for her. And since Dillon didn't bother to meet her—although it wasn't as if she'd told him what ferry she'd be on—why not ride with Jove? "How did you know I'd be here?"

"I arrived the day before yesterday and was disappointed that you weren't here anymore. I inquired when you'd return and waited."

"How long did you wait for me?"

He shrugged. "Not too long." He gave her a hand up and, once aboard, snapped the reins to get the horses in motion. "Have dinner with me tonight."

That didn't take him long. "I can't. I'm going to be occupied with wedding stuff until it's over."

He gave her a nod but looked disappointed.

At the hotel, her suitcases were taken off, but before she could step down, Jove took her hand. "Go for a ride with me before you get busy?"

It was best to keep her distance from him. "Thank you for the offer, but I really can't."

He released her hand. "If you find you have extra time, look me up."

Not going to happen. If she did find herself with extra time, it wouldn't be Jove she'd go looking for.

&

Dillon watched Aimee ride off with Jovan. He climbed into the carriage he'd borrowed from the hotel and drove back to the stable, then went to his office. He couldn't compete with Jovan. Jovan looked and acted the part of a movie star, and all the women treated him like one. Did Aimee find that appealing? He put his head in his hands. *Lord, what am I supposed to do?*

He startled at a knock on his door and looked up. *Aimee!*

"Hey, boss. I'm back."

His mouth pulled into a smile, and he stood. She'd come to see him and called him boss. Maybe she'd stay. "I'm glad you're here."

She gazed at the vase of pink carnations on her table-desk and sighed. "Are these for me?"

She liked carnations, didn't she? Steve said so. So why did

she look disappointed? "I hope you like them."

Her eyes widened. "They're from you?" She cupped the blooms in her hands and put her face to the flowers. She closed her eyes and drank in their fragrance. "I love the smell of carnations."

That was a relief. "I'm glad you like them." He came around his desk and gave her a kiss on the cheek.

She gave him a hug. "They're beautiful. Thank you."

He would do it a hundred times over to see her smile always like that. "Tell me about your grandma. How did she like the *treasure*?"

"She loved it. I don't think the treasure could have been any better for her. I also gave her the locket. She loves wearing it."

"So your time here was all worth it?"

"Every minute of it. I'm sorry I was such a bother to you."

"You were no bother." He nodded toward her chair. "I missed having you there."

"I missed being here. Anything exciting happen while I was gone?"

"As a matter of fact, yes." He crossed his arms. "Steve knocked on my door in the middle of the night asking about icebergs. What did you say to him?"

"So, what he and I talked about opened a door for you and him to talk? That's great. Is he any closer to accepting the Lord?"

"We talked for hours, and then he prayed. He's one of us now—a believer. I have been praying for him since the day I met him. This means a lot to me. Thank you." He stepped forward and hugged her.

"That's it! I just love it when the Lord shows me an answer to prayer." She whirled around and sat in her chair. "You remember before I told you why I'd really come? The whole Grandpa Wright stuff?" She waved a hand in the air and animated her explanation. "You were being so nice to me. I wanted to do something nice back. I asked God to show me something I could do for you. This is how God answered that prayer. Steve." Her smile broadened. "God is so awesome."

He was indeed. And if the Lord was willing, Dillon would see to it that Aimee remained in his life, somehow, someway.

&

Later that evening, Dillon sat across from Aimee at a table in the main dining room. Aimee wore a filmy black dress with wispy ruffles from the top down to her knees. The repeated rows of filmy waves reminded him of a flapper dress from the twenties. She looked great in it. He liked that she wore modest, below-the-knee dresses.

They'd had a pleasant meal, and Aimee seemed to be enjoying herself with him. Now was the time to ask her. He took a deep breath. "Will you watch the sunset with me?"

"So, while I was gone, you finally did it?"

He shook his head. "This will be the first time."

She sucked in a breath. "That is something between you and your mom."

"I want you there. I don't want to do this alone." He had tried alone. . .and failed.

She felt honored that he would want to share this moment with her. "Are you sure about this?"

He held out a hand to her and nodded. "If you'll go with me." He wanted desperately to share this personal moment with her.

She took his hand. "Of course."

He walked her out and west down the porch. He gripped her hand tighter as they approached the end of the porch. His lungs tightened, but he forced oxygen into them.

She gave his hand a squeeze. "Your mom would be so proud of you."

He loosened his hold on her hand but still held it firmly. "Thanks."

Pink, orange, and purple clouds were strewn across the sky, silhouetting Mackinac Bridge. Sunset was not always so colorful, he'd heard, but tonight was spectacular. He had finally done it. They stood in silence for nearly an hour watching the colors change and fade as the sunlight disappeared from the horizon.

Aimee turned to him. "Thank you for sharing this with me."

"No, thank you for being here for me. I don't think I could have done this without you. I can finally let her go." He waved a hand back toward the hotel. "And all of this, too."

"You're going to give up your job at the hotel?"

He took a deep breath. "If that's what God wants. I want to be where He wants me to be." For the first time in his life, he wanted God to be integral in all his plans.

Aimee knocked on the door of the modest house in Harrison-ville on the interior of the island.

A boy, a foot or so shorter than Aimee, answered the door. He wore a hockey mask and Rollerblades and carried a hockey stick. At least, she thought it was a boy.

"Is Susan here?"

The masked munchkin turned his head and yelled, "Mom, someone's at the door." He walked out onto the porch, rolled to the steps, and walked down them.

Aimee moved aside as two more miniature hockey players burst out the door and down the steps.

A chunky woman around forty came to the door. She held

up a finger for Aimee to wait and walked to the edge of the porch. "Carl, I'm not your mom."

The first boy turned back and pointed his hockey stick at Aimee. "She doesn't know that."

The woman shook her head. "Brian, be home by five." The woman turned to her. "Sorry about that. What can I do for you?"

"Are you Susan Cox? Formerly Susan Johnson?"

"That's me."

Aimee breathed a sigh of relief. She'd found the right place. "I work at the hotel with your father. Well, I don't exactly work with him, but we both work there. He is the sweetest man."

Susan smiled. "Dad's a charmer, that's for sure. He's told me about you. You're the 'cute little thing with an angel smile.' He's really taken with you, especially since you convinced Constance to marry him. Would you like to come in and have a glass of iced tea?" When she accepted, Susan poured the tea and led her out to the back porch.

A little girl was playing in the yard. She called to Susan, "Watch, Mommy, watch," then began to climb the short orange ladder of the plastic yellow slide.

"I'm watching." She kept one eye on the girl as she spoke to Aimee. "That's Lucy."

"So do you just have the two children?"

"I have five, ranging from five-year-old Lucy up to a twenty-year-old who just got engaged. My three older kids work the summer season here on the island, so I don't see them much. And then there is Carl, who spends most of his time over here. He jokes that I won't notice one more child and calls me Mom in the melee."

"It must be nice to have such a close family."

"It is, but some days, I'd like to take a vacation from them all. But where do you go when you live on a premier resort island and most of your family works the summer season and the kids have school the rest of the year?" She took a sip of tea. "So what brought you out this far from the cacophony of tourists?"

"I wanted to ask you a question about your sister."

"Cookie?"

"Is she going to make it for the wedding?"

"Oh, she is blustering a lot about the inconvenience, but she wouldn't miss it."

"How does she feel about your dad marrying Constance?"

"It depends on what day you talk to her. Her biggest argument is that she doesn't see a need for Dad to marry again at his age. What's the point? I think if it makes Dad happy for even two minutes, then he should go for it. I just never would have picked Constance Mayhew as a perfect match for him."

"Why not? They make a lovely couple."

"Oh, don't get me wrong. I like Constance. I'm glad she finally said yes. She's just a little more tightly wound than Dad is. She keeps him on his toes though, and he likes to tease her. I don't think she always appreciates his teasing, however. Can you just picture my little hockey player in her perfect house? It'll likely happen after they are married, but it will stress the poor woman out to no end. I'm sure she likes kids and all. She just never had any of her own. No experience."

"So you don't know how Cookie's going to react to the wedding?"

"Sometimes she is as cranky as all get-out, and other times she's just take-charge-Cookie, who can make things happen. The wedding could be hard for her because she has no control over it."

"But it's not her wedding."

"But she's Cookie."

So Cookie could go either way. Aimee remembered her older sister having fits to get her own way. Now, to see her so withdrawn. . . Was it another way of controlling?

 ❧

Gary, Henry's middle child and only boy, had come over from the mainland the day before the wedding with his wife and two kids and was staying at Henry's place. Cookie had booked a room at the hotel but still hadn't shown up. Aimee was staying with Constance until the wedding; then she would take a room at the hotel, which Dillon had reserved for her at Henry's request. Originally Henry had offered to let her stay at his place but had forgotten his son's family would be there. After the wedding, Aimee would likely leave the island for good. How could she go back to work with Dillon, day after day, and fall more in love with him, when he only saw her as a good assistant?

Constance stood in the bathroom fussing with her hair. Sammy sat on the toilet, watching every move she made. The phone rang. "Can you get that for me, dear?"

She answered it.

"Aimee?"

"Hi, Dillon."

"I just wanted to let Constance know that Henry's other daughter finally arrived. She just checked in."

It was about time. *Only an hour before the wedding!* "I'll tell her." She hung up and went over to Constance. "Don't panic, but—"

"Something happened to Henry." She panicked.

"Henry's fine. Cookie's here."

"Oh, good." Constance's shoulders relaxed. "To both."

"I thought you'd be stressed over having Cookie here."

"She's Henry's daughter. He would be disappointed if she didn't make it. I did some hard praying about it. If Cookie decides to cause a stir, I won't let it bother me. The wedding is in the Lord's hands. If it happens or not, it is up to the Lord." Constance really did look relaxed. "I hope Cookie can be happy for us. If not. . .then not."

"Wow. Is this the same woman who almost ripped her cloth handkerchief in half with her worrying?"

"It's amazing what prayer can do. And what good did worrying ever do? 'Don't worry about tomorrow. Tomorrow has enough troubles of its own.' Okay I'm still worrying a little. I do want her to like me."

An hour later, Aimee stood on her tiptoes to pin a hat with a short veil atop Constance's freshly styled hair. She was as beautiful as any bride could be.

Aimee wore a lavender dress and hat. "The carriage will be here in a few minutes." She stepped back. "You look absolutely beautiful. I hope I look as beautiful on my wedding day as you do now."

Constance turned to her with a wide smile. "Are you trying to tell me something?"

"Like what?"

"Like maybe that nice assistant hotel manager proposed to you?"

"Dillon? Marriage isn't in his five-year plan. And if it's not in the plan, it ain't gonna happen."

"He just needs to be sure of himself first."

"Dillon is always sure of himself. And he is sure that he is not getting married anytime in the near or distant future because it would deviate him from his goals." She heard the *clomp* of horse's hooves outside the open window and peeked out. "Your carriage awaits."

Constance took her cloth handkerchief and twisted it. "I'm suddenly nervous."

"Are you sure you want to marry Henry?"

"Very much."

"Then only think of him. The rest of us don't exist."

"But—"

"Eh, eh, eh. Only you and Henry."

Constance closed her mouth and picked up her bouquet. "Thank you for everything."

"I haven't done much."

"When you walked up my path that first day, I thought, *This girl is going to change my life.* I didn't know how. But it was all for the better. Thank you for stepping into my life. I was in such a rut that I needed someone else to pull me out."

She wished she could get someone else out of his rut. She opened the front door just as Dillon had his hand raised to knock. "You look beautiful."

"Thank you."

He turned to Constance. "Mrs. Mayhew—soon-to-be Johnson—I haven't seen a more beautiful bride."

"I bet this one would make an even more beautiful bride."

Aimee widened her eyes. "Constance!"

"Ah, that she might. I have come to escort the two of you to the wedding." He held out an arm to each of them.

Constance took Dillon's arm. "Come on, Sammy." Sammy trotted to her side. He looked adorable in his black bow tie.

Aimee locked the door and took Dillon's other arm. "We weren't expecting you to personally pick us up."

"Henry gave me strict instructions to make sure his bride got to the church. He didn't want her to get cold feet."

Constance huffed and climbed aboard the carriage. "How impertinent of him."

Aimee took Dillon's offered hand to climb inside and scooted next to Constance; then he followed, sitting next to her. She was dying to know about Cookie but didn't want to ask in front of Constance.

The wedding ceremony was small with only close friends and family. Sammy had sat patiently at Constance's feet. The lavish reception at the hotel was teeming with people. It seemed as though the whole island had turned out.

A woman with unnaturally red spiked hair greeted the bride and groom. Earlier Susan had identified her to Aimee as her sister, Cookie.

Aimee held her breath.

"Don't worry. She'll behave."

She turned to Susan who had silently come up beside her. Lucy sat on her hip picking at the ruffles on her dress.

"Daddy talked to her before the ceremony. She understands."

Cookie gave Constance a hug.

"I'm going to congratulate the newlyweds. It was nice seeing you again."

All seemed well, so she finally sat down at a table to rest her tired feet. Jove joined her and held out a cup of punch to her. She gladly took it. "Thank you."

"My pleasure." He draped one arm across the back of her chair. "I know you've been busy with all the wedding prep, but once all is said and done and the happy couple is off, I'd like to take you for a moonlight carriage ride around the island."

She took a sip of punch and set her cup on the table. "Jove, how do I tell you no without hurting your feelings? You have been very sweet, but I'm just not interested in that way."

He studied her a moment. "So you really aren't playing hard to get to see what lengths I'll go to woo you?"

She shook her head. "I don't think that's a fair game to play."

"An honest woman who honestly has no interest in me. Interesting. I wish I knew what I could do to change your mind."

"You would need to become a Christian for starters."

He pulled a face. "That would seriously cramp my style."

"Well, that's my style."

"If I could just change that one thing."

"You can't. God is permanent."

He removed his arm from the back of her chair and stood. "If you change your mind, I'm in the Garden Suite."

"I won't."

"Can you leave a guy with a little hope?"

"False hope?"

"Hope is hope." He walked away.

❧

Dillon watched again as Jovan occupied Aimee's attention. He wished he knew if she was just being nice to him or if she actually enjoyed his company. Jovan had a carefree charisma that women seemed to be drawn to.

Dillon knew that he had no such charisma. One couldn't plan charisma. And if it couldn't be planned, he couldn't do it.

"You watch her from a distance long enough, and one of these times you'll watch her walk right out of your life."

He turned and considered Katie's words.

She elbowed him. "What are you waiting for? If you like her, tell her."

Like didn't cover the gamut of emotions Aimee rocked in him. The one pulling out in front most would be labeled as *love*. But could Aimee be happy with him? He wasn't a free spirit like her. . .and Jove. He was bound by his plans. If he didn't plan, he felt lost. He felt lost without Aimee, too. But most of all, he wanted Aimee to be happy in her life. . .even if that life was without him.

fifteen

Aimee slipped off her shoes. It had been a beautiful wedding, but she was glad it was over and could rest her tired feet. She could almost hear her bed calling her. And she didn't have to travel over to Constance's house. Just a quick ride up the elevator. She pressed the UP button.

"Aimee."

She turned at her name.

Steve jogged toward her. "You aren't turning in, are you?"

"It's been a long day."

"I need you to come with me."

"Where?"

"It's a surprise. You might want to put your shoes on."

"Then I'm not going. My feet hurt."

"Fine." He grabbed her shoes from her hands and gave them a toss. "No shoes." He grabbed her hand and pulled her toward the front doors.

"Steve."

Carrottop Kevin opened the door with a big grin.

When she saw the carriage, she stopped short and gave a heavy sigh. *Jove.* "I'm not going." Jove had to understand.

Steve looked at her and back at the carriage. "You have to."

"No, I don't." She turned back toward the door.

Steve stepped in front of her. "Please. If you don't, I—I—"

"You what?"

"I could lose my job."

She rolled her eyes. "There is no way you would lose your

The Grand Hotel 161

job because I won't take a carriage ride."

Steve knelt down and pressed his hands together. "Please. Do me this one favor."

"I know what this is about, and I don't want to go."

"Then you know what a bad position I'm in. If you don't go, I'll pick you up and carry you to the carriage." He took her hand and pulled her toward the carriage. "Come on, you can do it. One foot in front of the other."

"You know, you are really annoying."

He gave her a big fake smile. "And proud of it. And I'll continue to be annoying until you get into that carriage."

What was the use? She heaved a big sigh. This time she wouldn't try to be nice. She would tell Jove no and that he had to stop pursuing her. She took Steve's hand to steady herself and stepped aboard. "I want my shoes."

"I'll be right back." Steve returned quickly and handed her shoes to her with a bow and a circular wave of his hand. "Driver, you may go now."

The carriage lurched forward and wound down Cadotte Avenue toward the water. She gazed up at the full moon, and her stomach twisted. She did not want to meet with Jove in some secluded place in the dark. How could she have let Steve push her into this?

"Driver, stop."

He pulled on the reins, and the horses eased the carriage to a stop.

"Take me back to the hotel."

The driver turned in his seat and took off his top hat. "But we're almost there."

"Dillon!" *What a relief.* "This was all your idea?"

"Whom were you hoping for? Jovan?"

"No, I was afraid it was him. He just doesn't take no for

an answer very easily."

"So you're not disappointed?"

Her mouth pulled into a smile. "Not at all."

"May I continue then?"

"Sure."

He snapped the reins and drove a little ways farther on the road. After setting the brake and looping the reins, he jumped down and gave her a hand to help her out of the carriage.

"Why didn't you just ask me to go for a carriage ride?"

"You were pretty stressed today over Cookie. I thought you might like a peaceful ride. I didn't think you would give Steve such a hard time." Dillon led her onto the beach.

She walked as much on her toes as possible and was grateful her heels weren't any higher. She didn't want to spoil this time by complaining about her shoes sinking into the sand. But they were filling up. She would take them off, but the sand was littered with rocks, about a fifty-fifty mix. She put a hand on Dillon's shoulder to steady herself. He stopped. She poured the sand out of one shoe and then the other.

He snapped his fingers. "I didn't think about your shoes. Do you want to go back to the carriage?"

"I'm here now. If I stand in one place, it won't be so bad."

He stepped around her and took her left hand and slipped his other hand into his pocket. "Remember when you asked me how I'd propose."

"Yes." It hadn't fit into his five-year plan. Maybe she needed to make her own five-year plan, a plan that would include him. No, that wouldn't work. Not only could she not even imagine how to start on a plan that long, but it would involve changing Dillon's plans, which seemed to be carved in stone. And if she did manage to alter his course in life, she would only drive him crazy with her lack of direction.

"You got me thinking. I think I would take my intended someplace alone, where it would just be the two of us, a romantic setting."

This was romantic. And they were alone.

"Perhaps a walk on a moonlit night."

She glanced up at the full moon and smiled.

"I would pull out my mother's wedding ring from my pocket." He pulled his left hand out of his pocket.

She stopped breathing.

"I would bend down on one knee"—and he did—"hold out the ring, and ask her."

Her hands began to shake.

"Aimee Mikkelson, will you marry me?"

She quickly raised her free hand to her mouth and accidentally hit his hand with the ring in it. Or rather, the hand that used to have the ring in it. She hadn't seen where it had flown. "Oh, I'm so sorry. I lost your mother's ring." She knelt down and started groping in the sand and rocks.

He grabbed her busy hands. "Here it is." Almost like magic, the ring was back in his hand.

She was sure she had seen it go flying. "How did you do that?"

He slid his fingers along a slender thread tied to the ring.

"You *planned* that I'd be a klutz and lose the ring?" She wasn't sure how to take that.

"No, I thought in my nervousness I'd drop it." They knelt face-to-face. "So will you marry me?"

He planned everything in his well-ordered life so he would succeed. Even to not lose his mother's ring. She stood and brushed off her knees. "You don't know what you are asking."

He stood, as well. "I'm asking you to spend the rest of your life with me. I thought you had feelings for me, too."

"Oh, Dillon, I do. Very strong feelings. And it is because of the love I have for you that I can't marry you."

He raked a hand through his hair. "That doesn't make any sense."

"I just don't think it would work out."

"The Lord is capable of mighty things."

"It's like a caged bird asking a cat to marry him. You are asking me, Miss Chaos herself, to be thrown into your perfectly ordered world. Have you thought about what that would do to all your well-laid plans?"

"It would add a little spice to them."

"Your life would be a mess. I don't plan hardly anything, and when I do, I often change those plans at the last minute. I can't go from no plans at all to having every minute accounted for. I like that you plan. There is a safety in it, a sense of security. It's part of what attracts me to you. But what could I give back to you but stress and headaches?"

Dillon's green-eyed gaze bore into her. "I don't want you to change. I need you just how you are. When my mom died, a piece of me died with her. I didn't realize how dead I was until you walked through the front doors of the hotel. You are like a breath of new life. Not the kind of eternal life the Lord gives, but like the sweet scent of June when the lilacs are in bloom. I feel as though the Lord is saying that I've mourned long enough. He's giving me another chance. There is something about the unknown that breathes life into everything. I want to change. Help me live again. Help me be more spontaneous. I can't give up planning altogether, but I can't remember doing one spontaneous thing since my mom died. She wouldn't want me to live like this. You have shown me that."

That was so beautiful. *But spontaneous?* "You really want to be spontaneous?"

"I'll prove it to you. Ask me to do something like you did that one time, and I failed. I won't fail this time." He gazed into her eyes. "Ask me."

Was he serious? "You're not going to hesitate but just do whatever I tell you to do?"

He nodded. "Whatever you say."

She could almost read in his look that he expected her to ask him to kiss her. "Wade in the water."

His eyebrows rose; then he smiled and turned toward the water.

"Aren't you going to take off your shoes first?"

"Nope. Too much planning and thought."

She grabbed his arm. "You'll ruin your shoes."

He squeezed her hand and removed it from his arm.

She grabbed his arm again. "I believe you."

"You are negating the spontaneity of the moment by detaining me." He scooped her up into his arms and walked out into the water.

"I can't believe you just did that. Is it cold?"

"You want to find out?" He loosened his grip on her momentarily, then tightened it.

She clutched him around his neck. "You're dangerous when you're spontaneous."

He gave her a wry smile. "I'm never spontaneous."

She glanced down at the water. "What do you call this?" It would only take him a second to release her from his stronghold.

"Plan B."

"You planned this?"

"If you were difficult, dumping you in Lake Huron was an option I considered."

"Well, please unconsider it."

"Will you marry me?"

"We've only known each other for six weeks."

"We'll have a long engagement."

"Are you sure?" She was sure about him.

"You know me better than most. I don't let people in easily. I'm not like your high school friends planning their weddings where all they needed was a name. There is only one name that can fit in the blank of my life—Aimee Mikkelson."

How could she say no when he was the only one to fit in her blank, as well? "Yes."

He kissed her as he waded out of the water and set her on the dry sand. He untied the thread from the ring, took her hand, and slipped it on her finger. "Now that you are going to be a permanent part of my life, I'd like for you to approve my new one-, five-, and ten-year plans."

"You made new plans already?"

"I don't function well without a plan. Maybe over the next fifty or sixty years, you can teach me how to live in the moment without a plan. But for now, I still need them."

"So in planning your life for the next ten years, you have also planned mine?" She wasn't sure how she felt about being locked into something for that long.

"Now that I have you, I'm not going to plan you out of my life."

She would have to get used to plans and schedules as a matter of course. How could she live that way? She could always have him plan to leave time open to be impulsive or at least follow her impulse. . .if he planned it. "Am I in all three plans?"

"Intricately."

"Then that is all I need to know. Don't tell me the details. Surprise me. That way, you can have your plan, and it won't seem like I'm locked into a schedule for the next ten years. It will seem unplanned to me."

A smile spread across his face, and his dimples pulled in. "I wasn't sure how our strong differences were going to mesh together and was leaving that one up to the Lord, but you have just worked it out." He picked her up around the waist and spun around. "I love you."

"I love you, too."

He kissed her again for a very long time.

epilogue

Two days after Labor Day

Aimee stood in the Grand Hotel lobby with her dad. "Thanks for being here and bringing Nonie to Mackinac Island."

He nodded. "I wouldn't miss my little girl's wedding. . .even if you did rush it."

"Dad, the only reason I wanted to get married so soon was so Nonie would be able to be here. She's doing well now, but things turn bad so quickly for old people. She's ninety-three!" Nonie's hip was nearly healed, far better and faster than the doctors anticipated for her age.

Her dad visibly relaxed.

She had thought Dillon was going to run as far from her as possible when she first brought up having an outdoor wedding by the end of the summer. He looked scared to death, like she'd just asked him to donate his heart and lungs to a needy person. He'd stayed up all night to create a plan. And she realized that his panic was because there was no plan for a wedding that soon. He made their wedding possible.

A hotel staff member came up to them. "They are ready for you down in the Wedding Garden."

Her dad turned to her. "You're sure he's the right one?"

"Positive."

He pulled the veil down over her face. "Then let's go."

She hooked her arm through her dad's. They walked out of the hotel, across the street to the top of the stairs that led to the hotel grounds. She picked up the skirt of Nonie's antique satin and bead dress to descend the stairs. The hanging beads tinkled as she walked. Nonie had guffawed at her calling the dress antique. Nonie said she wasn't an antique.

At the bottom of the stairs, Nonie in her wheelchair, Justin, Steve, and Constance waited. They went to the back of the gathering and lined up. The music changed, and Steve took Constance by the arm and led her up the aisle. At the front, Constance went one way, and Steve stood next to Dillon and his dad.

Nonie took Aimee's hand. "Don't be nervous, Muffin."

"I'm not, Nonie."

Nonie settled one hand on the side of the basket in her lap and the other into the pink rose petals inside it. Justin wheeled her down the aisle as she tossed the petals out in front of her. Nonie hadn't wanted to just be pushed down the aisle. She wanted something to do, so Dillon had come up with the idea of her being a sort of flower girl–matron of honor. Nonie loved the idea.

Finding the treasure had been the best thing to happen to Nonie and the rest of the family. Members who had ignored or avoided Nonie for years were suddenly visiting her. And now everyone lit around Nonie like fireflies. It had been too painful for the family to be around her and not believe. Now that the truth was out, the family had miraculously healed and come together. Well, most of them. There were still a few holdouts. *God can do the impossible and lavish you with treasure greater than you ever imagined.* Constance's words came back to her. She had never imagined the healing the Lord would do with that treasure. And so many of them had come. And during the middle of the week!

Justin parked Nonie next to Constance and took his seat.

The music changed, and everyone stood and turned toward her.

Her dad patted her hand hooked around his arm. "Ready?"

"I'm so ready I'd like to run up the aisle and throw myself into Dillon's arms." Walking just seemed so demure and sedate for the way she felt today.

Her dad chuckled. "I'll hold you back."

It took forever to reach Dillon at the front of the gathering His eyes shone with the love he had for her. The ceremony seemed to drag. She just wanted to be Mrs. Dillon Thurough. She didn't need any of the fluffy stuff. Finally the pastor pronounced them husband and wife, and Dillon gave her the sweetest kiss.

The pastor introduced them as Mr. and Mrs. Dillon Thurough. That was their cue to walk back down the aisle together.

She squeezed her husband's hand. "Let's run," she whispered.

He smiled and whispered back. "On three?"

"Three!" She took off running, leading Dillon, but soon he was pulling her.

A Letter To Our Readers

Dear Reader:

In order that we might better contribute to your reading enjoyment, we would appreciate your taking a few minutes to respond to the following questions. We welcome your comments and read each form and letter we receive. When completed, please return to the following:

Fiction Editor
Heartsong Presents
PO Box 719
Uhrichsville, Ohio 44683

1. Did you enjoy reading *The Grand Hotel* by Mary Davis?
   ❏ Very much! I would like to see more books by this author!
   ❏ Moderately. I would have enjoyed it more if

   _____

   _____

   _____

2. Are you a member of **Heartsong Presents**?   ❏ Yes   ❏ No
   If no, where did you purchase this book? _____

   _____

3. How would you rate, on a scale from 1 (poor) to 5 (superior), the cover design? _____

4. On a scale from 1 (poor) to 10 (superior), please rate the following elements.

   ____ Heroine   ____ Plot
   ____ Hero   ____ Inspirational theme
   ____ Setting   ____ Secondary characters

5. These characters were special because? _____

_____

_____

6. How has this book inspired your life? _____

_____

_____

7. What settings would you like to see covered in future
   Heartsong Presents books? _____

_____

_____

8. What are some inspirational themes you would like to see
   treated in future books? _____

_____

_____

9. Would you be interested in reading other **Heartsong
   Presents** titles? ❏ Yes ❏ No

10. Please check your age range:
    ❏ Under 18   ❏ 18-24
    ❏ 25-34   ❏ 35-45
    ❏ 46-55   ❏ Over 55

Name_____

Occupation _____

Address _____

City, State, Zip_____

wedded bliss?

4 stories in 1

In living out the daily business of life for 25 years, four couples seem to have forgotten the basics of for better, for worse, for richer, for poorer, in sickness or in health, to love and to cherish 'til death do us part. Is it too late to find wedded bliss?

Contemporary, paperback, 352 pages, 5³/₁₆" x 8"

_____

Presents